# MUST I WEEP FOR THE DANCING BEAR

## AND OTHER STORIES

# MUST I WEEP FOR THE DANCING BEAR, AND OTHER STORIES

by
Louis Phillips

PLEASURE BOAT STUDIO: A LITERARY PRESS
NEW YORK

"Must I Weep for the Dancing Bear," and Other Stories
By Louis Phillips

ISBN 978-1-929355-81-5
Library of Congress Control Number: 2012945561

Cover and Interior by Laura Tolkow, Flush Left



Pleasure Boat Studio books are available through the following:
SPD (Small Press Distribution) Tel. 800-869-7553, Fax 510-524-0852
Partners/West Tel. 425-227-8486, Fax 425-204-2448
Baker & Taylor 800-775-1100, Fax 800-775-7480
Ingram Tel 615-793-5000, Fax 615-287-5429
Amazon.com and bn.com

and through
PLEASURE BOAT STUDIO: A LITERARY PRESS
www.pleasureboatstudio.com
Email: pleasboat@aol.com

*For my sons*
*Matthew Louis Phillips*
*(1985-2011)*
*and*
*Ian Donald Phillips*
*With love*

*Acknowledgements:*

"The Black Messiah Cape" originally appeared in *South Dakota Review,* XII (Summer 1974)

"Must I Weep for the Dancing Bear" originally appeared in *The Yale Lit* (1975)

"Cubans" originally appeared in *The Nassau Review* (1981)

"Everything I Know about Lulu" originally appeared in *Wascana Review* (1982)

"The Man Who Was Struck by Lightning" originally appeared in *Inlet* (1985)

"Momma Went and Bought a New Pair of Shoes" originally appeared in *Whiskey Island Magazine* (Summer, 1987)

"Losses" originally apeared in *The DeKalb Literary Arts Journal* (1987)

"Real Crimes" originally appeared in *Oxford Magazine* (1989)

# TABLE OF CONTENTS

# CUBANS

About the owner of the sporting-wear factory, I don't remember his name. If I could remember the name of the factory, I bet the name of the owner would be part of it, but I cannot remember the name of the factory either. There is a good chance that I never heard the owner's name, because I was only a high school kid trying to earn money for college, and the owner…well, the owner was the owner. High school kids working for a buck sixty-two an hour don't talk to owners; we talk to foremen, and only if absolutely necessary. We hardly talked to each other. It was Florida. It was summer. It was a factory with no windows. And most of the employees were Cuban who had not learned English. It is difficult to feel good about oneself when you have so many things going against you.

To be completely honest, I don't remember one single name from the factory. A psychiatrist, I suppose, could make a big thing of that. Psychiatrists always like to tell people, for a goodly fee, how we suppress information about ourselves, important information, especially information revolving around unhappy times in our lives. It's a good theory, and I subscribe to it. I also subscribe to the notion that there are people who have bad memories. I am one of those.

You can ask me what the owner looked like, but I won't give you much of an answer. Besides, he doesn't figure very much in the story. He was a stoop-shouldered man with a bald head. He smoked cigars and wore a brown acrylic suit that even I, who did not have one single suit to my name, would have been ashamed to be seen in. He had retired at sixty-five, but he didn't know what to do with himself, so every morning at six he would limp into the factory, grab a container of coffee from the manager's desk, and then stand around and watch us punch in. It was the standard capitalist dream: the slave-owner and the darkies, the exploiter and the exploitee, the owner and owned. If he didn't have a factory to visit, I don't know what he would have done with himself. Tossed himself out of a window, I guess, the way his old lady had done during the Depression, and I don't mean his wife either. The sporting-wear factory was his beach house, his golf course, his cabin in the mountains. The stink of it, the cold of it, the noise of it, the terrible dead-end atmosphere of it. Some of the women who ran the sewing machines had been there ten to twenty years. Some of the cutters. Some of management. Some of the drivers. I had planned to remain only for the summer, but even that was going to be too much.

Of course there were teenage girls. A few. They modeled tennis outfits and short skirts and light-weight blouses. Perhaps the girls were the reason the old man held on to the factory with such bulldog determination. He didn't yell at me the way the manager did, but I hated him anyway. I hated him because he didn't pay any attention to me at all. I could have dropped dead at his feet, and it wouldn't have mattered. All he did was sip his coffee, sometimes drowning his cigar in the glop, and joke with the models. "Want to go to lunch with me, honey? I got no teeth. I thought maybe I could borrow yours. Or maybe we could just have Jell-O." He'd pinch their bottoms and they'd just smile at him. The models had freckles and straight teeth and breasts—oh, they had breasts—but they never joked with me. I knew at least two of them by name because they were in my class at school, but they didn't say much to me because I didn't own anything. I wasn't likely to own anything either. I was only the pimply kid with the sneakers, the bottle of Coke, and the brown eyes begging for mercy. I had a paperback book I kept in my back pocket – Susanne

K. Langer's *Philosophy in a New Key* – that somebody told me I should read, but there was never any time to read. There was a twenty-minute break at 10:30, but by the time I punched in and punched out and got settled, the whistle would blow. Besides, I wasn't going to let anybody see me trying to read such high-faluting stuff. There was one Cuban at the place who kept a stack of pornographic magazines on tap. Once you got a whiff of them, Susanne Langer could go put her head in a bucket.

And all the time there was the clackety-clack of the sewing machines, and the whirr of the cutting machines, which might have had technical names which I don't remember, and the fluorescent lighting banked overhead as if the hundreds of employees were thriving in some kind of a human greenhouse, a greenhouse without any glass at all, if you can imagine such a thing. It was like a super-long tennis court that had no nets. It was like a super deep swimming pool that had no water in it, no moisture at all, not even any sweat, for the air-conditioning made us forget that there was such a thing as Florida only a couple hundred yards away. It was always a relief, at the end of the day to walk outside and feel real air. Hot and humid, but real, and you could sweat in it all you wanted. It was like a motion-picture house where the same movie is shown over and over again, a movie that nobody ever wanted to see in the first place.

That was inside. And there were no blacks working out where I could see them. Because that's the way it was. In the early morning, when I walked to work, I watched the field across from the whatever-name-it-was factory. The field, glass-littered and weed-redundant, functioned as the town's unemployment office. Blacks gathered there before breakfast or perhaps instead of breakfast and waited for someone to drive up and offer them work. "I got a lawn that needs mowing. Any of you boys want to mow and rake? I'm offering seventy-five cents an hour? More'n most of you are worth." And maybe somebody would hop in, and off they'd go to do God-knows-what. Some of them I never saw again. Others would sit on their haunches and drink from paper sacks, then two of them would stand up and start sparring, and soon a circle would be formed, and then I'd go inside and forget about them.

When the factory let out at the end of the day, the same people would still be there, standing around, sitting on their haunches, breaking bottles over rocks, hoping that one of us would drop dead, or all of us. Sometimes we did.

I remember a woman back in the sewing area who suffered a miscarriage on the job. She was seven months pregnant and was bleeding heavily. When the ambulance arrived to carry the woman off, the manager was pissed. The whole work schedule had been thrown off. But even if one of us dropped dead, the factory owner would sooner hire a Cuban than a black man. Too expensive. Everybody understood that the owner had no intention of putting in separate toilet facilities or separate drinking fountains. That's just the way it was. A black Cuban was a philosophical problem that few people had stopped to consider.

The Cuban I worked with had a name I can't recall. However, I do remember that although I was only five foot eight, he was shorter than I was, and plump, with a chubby face and cheerful disposition. He wore glasses and was one of the cutters. He told me more than once that he had been a multi-millionaire at one time, but had lost everything when Castro came to power. When he fled with his family—a wife and four sons—all he took with him were the clothes on his back. Now here he was working in a factory once again, climbing on top of the tables to cut through layer upon layer of fabric that eventually would be sewn into tennis skirts and blouses. The cutters were the highest paid workers, but then their responsibilities were the greatest. The tiniest mistake, a simple deviation from the pattern, could cost somebody thousands of dollars and most likely cost the cutter his job. Still, my friend or quasi-friend didn't complain. Life was all one to him. That's the outstanding feature I remember about him. His lack of complaints, his equanimity, as it were, that and the loose gold sports shirt he wore day in and day out. Perhaps it was the only shirt he had. How was I to know?

When I say, however, that I worked with one particular Cuban, that is not entirely correct. I worked with them all. I worked with everybody in the factory, everybody, that is, except the models, for reasons I have explained. It was just that this one cutter in the gold shirt had shown me the ropes and sort of looked after me. God knows that if somebody hadn't looked out for me, I would have died at an uncommonly early age, most likely strangled to death by the foreman.

My work consisted of four major concerns: carrying and piling, piling and carrying, carrying and carrying, piling and piling. Minor concerns included tying cut fabric into small bundles for shipment to the sewers. It was important in somebody's book that the fabric be tied tight, for the material was tossed around, thrown into barrels. If the bundles were not tied correctly, pieces of cloth could go flying in all directions.

"Hey, college boy," the foreman barked at me during my second afternoon on the job, "tie up these bundles. Tie 'em good and tight. You can tie things good and tight, can't you?"

I nodded. Of course I could. Wasn't Houdini one of my all-time heroes? It took me all of twenty minutes to work my way from one end of the table to the other, picking up cut pieces, winding twine around them—not twine exactly, but not rope exactly, either, pulling the cord-like rope with all my might, adding a series of intricate knots not entirely unrelated to the Gordian.

As I was struggling through the final bundle, the foreman appeared at my left shoulder to inspect my work. "Got them tied good and tight?"

"Good and tight," I said. It was instinct that told me the best way to talk to a foreman is to repeat his words in some way. Still, he didn't smile at me, didn't acknowledge my existence one way or the other. He merely picked up one of the bundles, inspected it, sniffed, and tossed it overhand to a gaping barrel. The cut material broke free from their bonds and flew across the room in all directions, bits of brightly colored cloth parachuting through the air.

"Tight!" he said.

"I don't know what happened," I said. "Maybe the rope's no good."

"We've only been using it for the last twenty years." He turned toward one of the cutters. "Jose'," he called, "teach this smart kid how to tie a knot. He don't know how to tie things." To illustrate to the rest of the world at large, he picked up a second bundle from the table and tossed it through the air. It too fell apart. I could have fallen apart too, but I kept my mind on the fact that I wasn't going to stay in the factory forever. All I wanted to do was get through the summer and hot-foot it to New York, where fame and fortune beckoned. The foreman stalked off to his office, where the models were waiting, and didn't look back. If he had, he would have seen me blushing furiously.

Jose, who was as mean as they come, was grinning ear to ear. He scratched his head. "You want to learn to tie your shoelaces?" he asked.

"Yeah," I said.

"Smart college boys don't know how to tie nothing." And he taught me. There was a trick to tying a knot at the end of the rope and then making a loop with it. There were all kinds of tricks to be learned, but you always had to ask, or make a mistake first.

"You going to New York?" Jose' asked.

"Yeah." I guess my friend the cutter had told him.

"What for? What are you going to New York for?"

"I don't know," I said. "I'm just going."

"If you don't know what you're going for, you might as well stay here. No use going to New York if you don't know what you're going for."

"Maybe I'll find out when I get there."

"Not in New York. It's too big. You get lost there."

"I'm a writer," I said. "I'm going to New York to be a writer."

Jose' thought about it for a while. "A writer?"

"Yeah."

"Take my advice, kid," Jose' said, not taking his eyes off the bundle he was tying, "once you get out of this place, don't ever come back. Don't come back to this place for nothing." He pulled the cord tight and cut it with a razor. For the rest of the summer, he didn't make fun of me again. Soon everybody in the factory knew about my ambitions, for people kept coming up during the breaks or during lunch and they would press pieces of paper into my hand, crumpled up sections of cardboard with names, addresses, and phone numbers. Everyone had a relative or a friend in New York, someone I had to look up, someone who would give me a meal or a place to sleep.

My getting away meant a lot to my fellow workers, but it didn't mean a thing to my boss. The foreman always came up with new ways to humiliate me. Of course, it wasn't always his fault.

After I had set a new record for tying bundles, the foreman took it upon himself to broaden the scope of my responsibilities. I was singled out to operate the pattern-duplicating machine.

Inside a small room not more than thirty feet away from the cutting tables stood an eight-foot object—brown, menacing, coiled, polished, and plugged. To me it looked like a guillotine. "Pay attention, College Boy," the foreman said. "You see this pattern?" He held some tissue-thin paper under my nose. I couldn't miss it if I had wanted to. "It takes twenty-four hours or more to draw these things, so God help you if anything happens to it." I had no reason to doubt his word.

He approached the machine. I thought he genuflected, but that was merely my imagination working overtime. He unrolled the first eight inches of tissue-thin pattern, smoothed the paper carefully. Soon the pattern began to unroll, drawn into the bowels of the duplicator. We waited. I wasn't bored exactly. From the top of the machine, heavy copy paper made its appearance. I could make out the hieroglyphics as the foreman grabbed the copy and tore it straight across, using a piece of wire that had been stretched across the middle of the machine for such a purpose. We waited. Finally the paper-thin original appeared. The foreman carefully gathered it in, rolling it ever so slowly around a piece of long cardboard.

"Got it?"

"Got it," I said. I hadn't, but what the hell. I wasn't planning to spend the rest of my life making copies of patterns. Besides, I had learned early on not to ask the foreman for anything. He believed in showing someone a procedure once. Once was enough. That was his motto. Besides, with any luck, I wouldn't be called upon to run many patterns. I had more important things to do, such as learning new jokes to keep the cutters entertained along with the women behind the sewing machines. I was a single-minded anti-suicide squad. My plan was to remain out of sight on the far side of the building.

Like most of my plans, it didn't work. Who can forget Lennie and the rabbits in *Of Mice and Men*? Eventually the hue and cry went up: "College Boy? College Boy? Where in the hell is he? College Boy, get over here! I'm tired of looking all over the building for you."

I did as I was told. The foreman screwed up his face and thrust a new pattern into my outstretched hand. "Make a copy of this and deliver it to Jose'. Got it? Give the machine time to warm up," he said, walking away.

Two months, I thought. Is two months long enough for the machine to warm up? I entered the room—in In Cold Blood, Capote would have called it "the Corner"—and turned the machine on. It hummed. The electricity punched in and did its work. I carefully unrolled the pattern on a stainless-steel counter and I smoothed the tissue-thin paper. I smoothed it and smoothed it. I smoothed it again. I held it up to the light and examined it for any imperfections. I couldn't think of anything else to do, so I rolled the pattern back onto the roller. Unrolled it again. Smoothed it, then, holding my breath, I fed it into the machine. The machine gurgled happily. I looked up just in time to see paper pouring forth. The machine had been storing paper for centuries. It had simply required my magic touch to release it. Paper was pouring over my head with a vengeance.

Aside from the duplicating paper pouring down in a steady stream, the only other sound was the crinkling and crumpling of the original. With heady indifference, the copier was laying a heavy hand upon the pattern, lapping it and folding it, adding wrinkles and creases where creases and wrinkles had no business being. I had done something wrong, but I was afraid to turn off the machine. An abrupt halt, I thought, might tear the original; then where would I be? I waded through a pile of paper and shut the door. The interior of the cubicle resembled an ice-floe. It was no longer a solitary room; it was an Arctic region of white tissue. In short, I was not happy.

There was a light rap upon the door. Edgar Allan Poe could not have done it any better. I sprang forward, but the door pushed open, and my Cuban friend in his loose gold shirt poked his chubby face inside. "You're in trouble, aren't you?" he said.

"Who? Me?"

"Yes, you, amigo." He pushed the door open, entered, and closed it. He surveyed the wreckage and whistled. "You do this, amigo? All by yourself?"

"No, I had help. God helped."

My friend pushed back his glasses and rubbed his eyes. His eyes had been giving him trouble. "Ah, yes," he said. "God is good at creating messes. Now what are you going to do?"

"I'm going to go to New York."

"Right now?"

"Should I stay here and let the foreman kill me?"

My friend pointed his thumb over his right shoulder. "Get José. Tell José to come in here, and you stand outside the door. You keep guard."

"I don't want you to get into any trouble on my account," I said. I meant it, but I didn't mind him helping.

He shrugged. "If the cutters don't get the patterns, we'll all be in trouble. If you see the foreman coming this way, knock on the door three times."

"And then what will you do?"

"Blame everything on you."

On that cheery note I left. I explained my situation to José, and José, grinning ear to ear, went off to the room. He was not entirely unpleased that I had shown myself to be incompetent. I stood outside the door and listened to the music that was playing softly overhead. I was confused. There was no doubt that I had to pretend I was working and standing guard, but I couldn't think of anything to do. There was no activity where I was standing. I tied my shoes eleven times.

From all the way across the long room, I could hear the foreman's voice. "Hey, College-Boy, you got those patterns?"

I nodded. "Got them," I said.

"Well? Where are they?"

Nobody even looked up from the tables. Everyone was used to being shouted at. "Inside," I called back. "I didn't know where you were." If I was learning anything from my stint in the factory, I was learning to lie like a lawyer.

"Well, you do now," he shouted. I nodded. I certainly did. "Don't just stand there. Get them for me. And be careful with the original. If anything happens to that, it's your neck.

I smiled. I nodded. I opened the door to the cubicle and slipped inside. Jose' and my friend were stretched out upon the floor. Using the weight of their bodies, they were trying to flatten the original pattern back into shape.

"He wants the patterns," I told them.

"Who?"

"Who do you think?"

"He's going to have to wait," my friend said. His tan shirt was wringing wet.

"I've got to give him something," I said.

"Give him this," José answered, making an obscene sign with his fingers.

"Very funny," I said. "What am I going to tell them?"

"Where is he right at this minute?" my friend asked.

"How do I know?"

José stood up. He was enjoying my discomfort. "Open the door and peek out. Or maybe you have X-ray vision like Superman."

I did as I was told. The foreman, thank God, was still on the far side of the room. He and the owner were flirting with the models. "They're flirting with the models," I told them.

"I wish I was flirting with the models" José said. José was

married. His wife, in fact, worked in the sewing division. But it didn't matter to him. My quasi-friend stood up and said something in Spanish. I didn't understand. I had been there two months and I still didn't know any Spanish. He crossed to the copying machine and fed it the original. "Watch," he told me, "so you'll know next time. I can't be saving your neck all the time."

"When you become a citizen," I said, "you can use me for a reference."

"You'll be in New York. What good will you do me in New York?"

"What good will he do anyone in New York?" Jose' added.

I watched. The machine behaved itself. The paper-thin original, slightly worse for wear, ran through, and out poured a copy. I sighed. José was stuffing wads of paper under his shirt and up his pants legs, and was urging me to do the same. "Put some of this trash under your shirt," he said, "and when you pass a trash basket get rid of it."

"Thanks," I said. When the duplicate pattern was duly torn free from the machine, I grabbed it and ran out. The waste paper under my shirt scratched my stomach.

That night, with the shades of Ebenezer Scrooge and Silas Marner hovering over me, I counted my money. Two hundred dollars. Was there ever a man as rich as I? A good friend of mine had been hired to teach at some Lutheran high school on Long Island. He told me that he would drive me north, drive me from the Land of Slavery to the Land of Freedom, and not even charge me for gas. He had rented a small apartment, and I could stay with him. Under such conditions, two hundred dollars could last forever.

When I gave notice, the foreman didn't look me in the eye. "You can't take it, can you?" I didn't answer. "I've been here for thirty years, and you can hardly last three months. What's the matter? You got no guts?" I didn't say anything. He took my timecard out of the clock and studied it. "I suppose you expect to have your last paycheck in hand when you walk out these doors?"

"It would be nice," I said.

"Tough. We don't break the rules for anybody. Especially not for hot-shot college boys." He pushed a new pattern into my hands. "Run me off three copies," he said. "And don't take all day like you did last time." He walked away. "Christ, New York! You won't last five minutes in New York."

The day I left was a Saturday, for that was the half-day shift. We all got out at two, and my friend was waiting in his brand-new Chevrolet. His father was a banker. He had money, and I had money. I had two hundred dollars. I had stuck most of it into my sneakers so it made me walk funny. Nobody said much. Not the foreman, nor José, nor my quasi-friend in his gold shirt. A tiny woman with a skin like leather had given me three postcards from the 1939 World s Fair. She worked in the sewing department.

"I don't think the Fair's still on," I told her. "It was over a long time ago. Before I was even born."

She nodded. She didn't speak English very well. I placed the cards in my shirt pocket, picked up my cardboard suitcase, a suitcase that had once belonged to my grandmother, and I gave the time clock a good rap with my fist. When I walked outside, she followed me. Hell, everybody followed me. By the time I reached the parking lot, the sidewalk was crowded with Cubans. As I climbed into the car, they just stood around and watched. The cutters. The sewers. The tiny woman with the leather skin. The errand boys.

"What you got?" my friend asked. "A parade?"

"I dunno."

There were about two hundred in all. I tossed the suitcase into the backseat and waved. The car lurched forward, and I almost lost my balance. And then we were leaving the parking lot, and the Cubans were running after us. A couple of them were shouting, but I didn't know Spanish, so I don't know what they were saying.

# THE REVENGE OF FRANKENSTEIN

"Cursed, cursed creator! Why did I live? Why, in that instant, did I not extinguish the spark of existence which you so wantonly bestowed? I know not; despair had not taken possession of me; my feelings were those of rage and revenge. I could with pleasure have destroyed the cottage and its inhabitants and have glutted myself with their shrieks and misery."

Percival Lubbock glanced up from the thick leather book he had been reading: *The Boy's Book of Horror Tales and Poems*. He had been attracted to the volume in his father's library because of a movie advertisement he had seen in the *Gaffney Sun*. The stories, however, were too difficult for his ten-year-old mind. Many of the words were long and strange; many of the stories were complicated. Still, he enjoyed studying the black-and-white illustrations, especially the one that showed a sailor with a white albatross hung about his neck.

"I got the money!" Justine announced triumphantly. Justine was Percival's sister. She was eight years old, blonde, and tidy. He had sent her on the movie-money errand. "But you have to promise to sit through the whole movie whether you like it or not," Justine insisted.

Percival made a face and held out his hand for the quarter. It would cost fifteen cents to go to the movies. The extra ten cents would be for the bus ride home.

"Don't make any faces at me, PJ. The last time we went, you made me leave before it was over." Justine removed the box of Cheerios from the kitchen table. She stood on a chair to put the cereal box into the cupboard and then climbed down She walked into the living room to fetch her school books. Percival, or PJ, which everyone called him (his middle name was John), pocketed the quarter, closed the big leather book, and waited for his sister to return. Together they walked from the house to the bus stop at the end of their block. The red ground around the crude wooden bus shelter was always muddy. Even on days when there was no rain, the ground remained red and muddy. His sister hated the mud. It ruined her shoes, she said. PJ could never get excited over shoes.

By the time the bright orange bus arrived, Percival had formulated his plans for the day. *Frankenstein*, the very story he had been reading at the breakfast table, was playing at the Palace. When school let out at noon, as it always did on the day before Thanksgiving, Percival and Justine would not take the school bus home. Instead they would walk from the school into town. PJ had told his sister that the movie was a Western, but she would soon find out what kind of a movie it really was. He hoped it would scare her. It would teach her a lesson. A good lesson.

Unfortunately, PJ's plans did not work out the way he had expected. When the monster on the screen came alive, PJ looked away. When the monster lured the young girl to the lake and drowned her (a young girl who looked a lot like Justine), PJ gasped. His chest hurt. His small fingers scratched at the armrest of his chair. Then there was no air at all in his lungs. He felt the need to go to the bathroom, but he was afraid to get up.

Justine shook her head. "You promised," she told him. She didn't even look at her brother.

"I don't like it." He tried to sound matter-of-fact.

"Well, I do," she said, scrunching down into her seat.

The old man sitting directly behind PJ told the children to be quiet.

"I want to go home," PJ pleaded.

"No," Justine said firmly. "I want to stay."

PJ groaned. The man behind them told them that if they didn't stop talking he would call for the manager.

"You promised," Justine whimpered. She refused to take her eyes from the screen. Two teen-age boys sitting in the very front row of the Palace were laughing loudly and tossing pieces of popcorn toward the lurking hulk on the screen. An usher came down the aisle and told the teenagers to sit up and behave. One of the boys made a rude noise.

"We're going," PJ said.

"If you make me go," Justine told him, "I'll scream. I'll scream and kick."

Percival was sweating. He did not want his sister to make a scene. She would embarrass him. She would call him names. She would tell everybody how frightened he had been. On the screen, men with torches were chasing the monster. The monster was trying to escape. He made brute animal noises. But PJ did not feel sorry for the monster. He hated the monster. The monster had done bad things, and now he would be punished. He should be punished for his crimes. PJ felt a trickle of fluid down his pants leg. In fear and humiliation, PJ began to cry.

Justine still refused to leave. She made PJ sit through the film until its bitter end. By the time they left the Palace, PJ felt sick to his stomach.

"The bus stop's this way," Justine said, but PJ walked in a different direction. Justine followed. By way of revenge, PJ forced his sister to walk all the way home with him. Of course, it was revenge upon himself also. Revenge for being a crybaby. Revenge for wetting his pants. Revenge for choosing the movie in the first place. Revenge for bearing through life, like a talisman against ever growing into manhood, a name like Percival. The Knights of the Round Table meant nothing to him. Nor did the dusty brown book in the kitchen.

The walk from the movie theater to home was far from pleasant. At every corner, behind tall bushes, behind the trunks of oak trees, hidden in the tall grass, lurked a tall man in a dark blue suit. The man was scarred from head to foot. He walked with a terrifying stiffness. PJ walked faster and faster. So did Justine. In the movie theater, Justine had kept her fears at arm's length; but in the fading afternoon sun, she was no longer confident that Frankenstein's creation did not exist. The children repeatedly glanced over their shoulders and ran and ran and ran. The solitary dime that had been destined for the bus remained clutched in Justine's right hand.

At dinner, PJ's father erupted into fury. "Who allows children into such movies?"

Justine's mother turned her back to the kitchen table. She stood at the sink and pretended to study the huge turkey that was defrosting in the sink. "They told me they were going to see a Western," she said quietly. Tomorrow there would be so much to give thanks for.

"You think *Frankenstein* is a Western! My God, what kind of a woman did I marry?"

"They didn't tell me it was *Frankenstein*," Adele said. She dabbed her eyes with her apron.

"The movie wasn't scary, Daddy," Justine said. "It wasn't scary at all. Honest."

Warren glanced at his daughter. She didn't say anything more. PJ stared at his dinner plate and began to cry.

"Oh God!" Warren said. "This family is driving me crazy." He left the room. He walked with a limp. A friend of his had accidentally shot him in the left leg during a deer hunt.

Late that night, snow began to fall, and the entire world was on fire. At least it seemed that way. PJ was in a haystack, and the hay was burning, or maybe he wasn't PJ Maybe he was his sister. A barn door slid open, and silhouetted in its entrance was a man that looked like PJ's father. And then the man was a stranger. And then the man was on fire.

"...I entered a barn which had appeared to me to be empty. A woman was sleeping on some straw; she was young, of an agreeable aspect, and blooming in the loveliness of youth and health. Here, I

thought, is one of those whose joy-imparting smiles are bestowed on all but me. And then I bent over her, and whispered. 'Awake…'
PJ screamed.

As he was fighting off the fire, PJ's mother came running toward him. She took him in her arms and comforted him. His father paused briefly at the door to his son's bedroom. In striped pajamas without any top, he appeared to be lost. He stood with his arms folded across his hairy chest and cursed. PJ's mother stayed with her son until he fell back asleep, fell safely beyond the boundaries of the fire.

On Thursday afternoon, the Greek sea captain appeared. One of the local charities, responding to an invitation from PJ's parents, had sent him. PJ greeted the man at the door. The man mumbled something. His name turned out to be Elytis. Elytis Karos. He was in his middle forties, but he looked decades older. He was dressed in a heavy blue coat that reeked of pipe tobacco. PJ did not like the man, and he did not like the idea of spending Thanksgiving with someone he did not know, even though his parents had warned him, had told him and Justine that there were a lot of people in the world not as fortunate as themselves. It was an experiment, PJ's mother had said. PJ no longer possessed any affection for the word *experiment*. After what he had seen, the word *experiment* meant only horror to him.

The stranger weighed nearly three hundred pounds. He was a rotund man with a mass of gray hair and a beard that hadn't been combed. There were bread crumbs in it, or some kind of crumbs. A small cap perched precariously on the top of the man's head, a sea-captain's cap of some sort.

When the man entered the Lubbock household, PJ and Justine stared wide-eyed. He carefully maneuvered himself through the narrow doorway. PJ, embarrassed, looked away. Justine smiled. She hoped that he would get stuck in the door frame. It would be great fun, she thought. They could bring him his meal, and he could eat standing up, jammed between the wooden frames of the tiny door.

The entranceway of the house had never looked so small before.

The stranger entered the house. He had brought nothing, but PJ concluded that he had nothing to bring. He was a "charity case," his mother had told him. PJ had never seen a charity case before. His parents had mentioned that he was a reformed alcoholic, and that's all they knew about him.

"This is PJ and Justine, and I'm Warren," PJ's father said, "and this is my wife, Adele."

"We're so happy to have you here," Adele said, beaming. She held out her hand, but the man did not take it. He made a subtle bow at the waist, and nodded his head.

"Down at the Seaman's Chapel, Father Skyros wrote out your address for me." He rummaged in the huge pockets of his coat, fumbling for a piece of paper. He found it, held it forth triumphantly. When he smiled, the children saw that he had only a few yellowed teeth. Many teeth were missing.

"I hope you didn't have any trouble finding the place," Adele said. She took the piece of paper from the man and, not knowing what to do with it, placed it neatly on the coffee table.

"We want you to know that we are happy to have you here for Thanksgiving, and we want you to make yourself at home. Let me get you something to drink."

Adele stared at her husband. Finally she told Justine to help the man with his coat. Justine did as she was told, but when she carried the coat to the hall closet, she held the garment as far from her body as she could.

"And your hat, Mr. Elytis?" Adele asked.

"Karos," Warren corrected her, and held out his hand for the man's cap. The stranger merely removed it and held it in front of his chest like a tiny shield.

"Something to drink?" Warren repeated.

"I'm just fine," Mr. Karos said, nodding at PJ "Just fine. You have such a lovely home. Such lovely children."

"Won't you sit down?" Adele suggested.

The man sank into the sofa. Both ends of the sofa seemed to rise up to greet him.

"You mustn't be bashful," PJ's mother said. "We have so much more than we can possibly eat. More than we can possibly know what to do with. So you just make yourself at home here. You have to know that you're doing us a favor by coming here. Otherwise all this food would go to waste." She pushed a bowl of olives toward him.

"My coat," the man said, almost apologizing. "I forgot to take out my pipe, please. And my pouch."

"Justine, bring our guest his pipe," Warren said.

"And pouch, please."

Justine sighed and went back to the closet and retrieved the pipe and leather tobacco pouch.

"If you'll excuse me, Mr. Karos," Adele said, emphasizing his name for her own benefit, "I have to get dinner ready. You must make yourself comfortable, and don't let the children bother you." She retreated to the kitchen. Justine ran after her mother.

The man unzipped the pouch and filled his pipe.

"Are you sure we can't offer you something to drink," PJ's father said, looking bereaved. "We have soft drinks, fruit punch, whatever you like." His voice trailed away. He started to sit down in his usual chair, but quickly stood back up.

"I had to give up hard drinking," Mr. Karos said. "It's what has brought me to my fallen state. That and a woman." He was boasting slightly. He shifted his weight on the sofa, and lit his pipe. The air was soon tinged with a heavy tobacco odor. PJ didn't go near the man. Instead he hung back and fooled with the large black knobs of the big Philco radio that dominated the living room.

"You been in the South a long time?" PJ's father asked.

The Greek shook his head. He removed the pipe from his mouth, thought a moment, and then said, "I'm never anywhere very long. There are three countries," the man said: "the land of the living, the land of the dead, and the sea. I prefer the sea, especially the Arctic regions. I love the Arctic. It's so cold and desolate. But clean. Pure. So white, so white. It's nice to go to places where no one has ever really set foot. But here it's too hot all the time. Too hot." His face was perspiring. He wiped his forehead with his sleeve. "It's hot in Greece, too," he added, "but not in the same way."

During the Thanksgiving dinner, Adele asked the man if he had any family, and the man said, "No. My parents are both dead."

"I'm sorry to hear that," Adele said. "More turkey?"

The man held out his plate. On the back of the man's left hand was a tattoo of a heart with the initials J.L. written inside it. Both children noticed the tattoo. They really paid attention to how much food the man ate. They felt that the man was taking something that belonged to them. Warren sat at the head of the table and tried to think of things to say. Adele hopped up and down, checking and rechecking the oven. "I think something's wrong with my oven," she said.

"My father burned himself to death," the Greek said matter-of-factly. "He was cleaning his coat with kerosene, and he got too close to the furnace. I was only ten at the time. The flames seemed to leap out and eat him alive. It was the most horrible thing I had ever seen in my whole life. My father screamed and started rolling on the floor. I screamed and yelled and jumped up and down. I grabbed a blanket from my bed and threw it over him and tried to smother the flames. My mother was downtown shopping at the time, and so I ran to the neighbors and they called an ambulance. And you know what? There was a strike on. Some of the hospital workers were on strike, and they wouldn't let the ambulance out of the parking lot. Those bastards!" The stranger was gesticulating wildly. A knife in one hand, a fork in the other. PJ's mother blanched at the man's language. "Those bastards wouldn't let the ambulance out of the parking lot," the man roared. "I swear I'm going to get my revenge upon them someday."

The Greek sailor stopped. Justine, with wide-eyed admiration, stared at the man. PJ began to cry. Great tears welled up in his eyes, and he couldn't hold them back.

"I'm sorry," the stranger said. "I got carried away." He lowered his head.

"It's quite all right," Adele answered, removing the gravy bowl from the table. "But this is Thanksgiving. We must try and concentrate on the good things. Yes, on the good things."

The stranger placed his fork down upon his empty plate and carefully laid his knife across it. The instruments formed a metallic cross. "I didn't mean to upset the boy."

Flushed with anger, Warren glanced at his son. "I don't know what's gotten into him lately," he said. "Get away from the table," he ordered PJ. "I don't want to sit at the same table with a crybaby. A crybaby is no son of mine."

Adele returned to the table. "Oh, leave the boy alone, for land's sakes," she told her husband. She sat down. "PJ was up all night with nightmares. He's overtired, that's all, and your story set him off. Can't we talk about something else?" she pleaded.

Mr. Karos held out his tattooed hand and rumpled the boy's hair. "I'm the one who should be crying, not you," he said. PJ pulled away from the stranger's touch.

"Take a sip of milk," Adele advised her son.

PJ stopped crying. Warren shook his head.

"I liked *Frankenstein*," Justine announced. "It didn't give me no nightmares at all."


*"Slave, I before reasoned with you, but you have proved yourself unworthy of my condescension. Remember that I have power; you believe yourself miserable, but I can make you so wretched that the light of day will be hateful to you. You are my creator, but I am your master;—Obey!"*


Several weeks passed. One day shortly before Christmas, the Greek sailor, in his same coat, bearing with him his identical bulk in the world, returned to the Lubbock household. He had not been invited. His arrival was entirely unexpected. This time he brought with him no single crumpled sheet of paper with an address scribbled upon it. Instead he plucked from his dirty pockets an assortment of letters tied together with string. He and PJ's parents read the letters, and they sat in the dimly lit kitchen and talked. The talk went on for many hours. PJ remained upstairs and tried to overhear the muffled words. By the time Mr. Karos left, the kitchen reeked with tobacco and garlic and foreignness. Foreignness above all.

And then the parents talked. Warren raised his voice, and Adele finally walked upstairs to Justine's room to confront her daughter.

"Perhaps you can explain these letters, young lady," Adele demanded.

Justine's eyes grew round as saucers. "What letters, Momma?"

Adele blushed. "You know very well what letters. These letters. These love letters that you have been writing every day to Mr. Karos!"

"Mr. Karos?"

"The man who spent Thanksgiving with us."

"Why would I write him, Momma? I haven't been writing him letters. Honest. Cross my heart and hope to die."

Adele sat down upon her daughter's bed. She took her daughter's hands and gently massaged the backs of them. "You wouldn't lie to me, would you, Darling. This is very serious business. Very serious. Your father and I are very upset about this, because it is a very terrible thing to make fun of somebody like this."

"Make fun of who, Momma?" Justine, in all innocence, asked.

She was frightened. Very frightened. She had never seen her mother quite so muted. "Can I see the letters, Momma?"

"I don't want you to read them if you didn't write them."

"I just want to see the writing, Momma."

Adele untied the packet, withdrew a letter, and opened it. The letter had been crudely typed upon tissue-thin paper. "Mr. Karos is very hurt that somebody is making fun of him."

Justine started to cry. "No, Momma. I didn't make fun of him. Honest."

Adele sighed. She clasped her weeping daughter to her bosom.

"I believe you, Honey. I believe you. We'll get to the bottom of this somehow."

Across the hall, PJ sat on his bed. Through the opened doors he could see Justine and his mother. The small lamp on Justine's night table cast two huge weeping shadows on the wall.

# LOSSES

Deep-in-Despair, for all you chroniclers of America's sweethearts and losers, was born Edward Hauser MacAdoo in 1928 on the nose of Chickamauga Lake, Tennessee. However, he had just turned fourteen when his old man bundled the family off to Saratoga Springs. It was at Saratoga Race Track that the real drops of sour slipped down his throat and forever bittered him.

It seems that Ed's old man, who peeled potatoes and did odd jobs for the old Saratoga Inn, had a day off coming to him and, in the spirit of conscientious fatherhood, decided to spend some time with his eldest son. Ed's old man, who was named Clinton, was tinkering with the family car in the front yard. Ed shuffled into the house to fetch a sweater out of his father's closet, when Ed's mother collared him.

"Edward?"

"Yeah?" Ed knew he was in trouble because his mother used the full two syllables. If wallet photos mean anything, Ed's mother was a real hatchet-faced job. She was some six or seven years older than her husband and had given birth to Ed late in her career. Not that the snapshot did her no good.

"Don't say *yeah* like that, young man. Just who do you think you're talking to?"

"Sorry," Ed mumbled.

"Say 'Sorry, Ma'am.'"

Ed glanced past her and out the window. He was a trapped beast. "Yes, ma'am." His voice was barely audible. "Dad's waiting." He had hoped those last two words would solve everything.

Mrs. MacAdoo raised her left hand to her forehead and squinted at her son. "I know he's waiting," she said matter-of-factly. "Where's he taking you?"

"I don't know."

His mother's mouth tightened. "He's taking you to the race track, isn't he?"

Ed shrugged. From outside came the sound of the car horn. "I gotta go," he said.

His mother reached out and touched him on the shoulder. She rarely touched him. "Well, you go, son, and you have a good time with your father. But you watch him. You know what I mean? He's got his week's salary with him, and the rent is due. And old man Holley is up in arms about the grocery bill. You know what I'm telling you, son?" She leaned in close to me, her face twitching. "You're the sensible one. He'll listen to you. If he starts losing, you get him away from there. We need the money. You understand?"

Ed nodded. He understood. He broke loose from his mother's grip and ran outside and leaped upon the running board in James Cagney fashion. If Deep-in-Despair could have been anybody in life, my bet is that he would have chosen James Cagney. But then, who wouldn't?

The weather was fine and the track was fast. Clinton explained to his son how to read *The Morning Telegraph*, showing him how to tell a good jockey from an average one, which trainers to respect, how to use past-performance figures. In school, Ed was a wizard in math, and there in the sun, with the smell of dust and mowed hay, math was a touchstone for two very different people.

Ed's father, a balding man with reddish-brown moustache, never earned much money, but he dressed well. Hardly anybody ever saw him without a suit and tie. Above all, he kept his Ford in mint condition. He loved cars and horses and a good head of foam on his beer. He was inclined to telling racy stories, which made his son blush. *The Morning Telegraph* was soon covered with neatly inked figures, numbers written in a hand so fine that they cried out to be read through a magnifying glass.

In spite of early losses, Clinton was expansive. He bought his son red-hots and beer, and with the sun breathing down, there was something more than religion at work, especially when the thoroughbreds were pounding down the stretch, heading neck and neck for home, with everyone in the stands—prince and pauper, governor and commoner—cheering for their own; and the two of them—father and son—standing shoulder and shoulder, the son now as tall as the father, leaning forward, shouting, then giving little leaps off the ground, desperate dancers that they were, then turning away, hitting the wooden railing with disgust, waiting for the official results on the tote board, and the numbers slashing, and then tearing up the tickets and scattering the pieces like confetti over the yard.

Clinton, in a burst of generosity, had even given his son a five-dollar bill so that Ed could have the luxury of going his own way on several bets. In the fourth, Ed, his head beginning to lightly hum from the bucket of beer, plunked down the fiver on a three-year-old named Chickamauga.

It was a hunch bet all the way down the line. Clinton scoffed, pointing out, the veins rising in his neck, how the nag was way outclassed. The son had second thoughts about going against his old man's choice—a chestnut named Betty Be Good—so Ed put the money to show.

Ed's bet violated two of Clinton's basic rules. One, never bet with scared money, and Ed had been made scared by his mother's last-minute warnings. Two, never bet a horse to show. What's the sense of gambling if you're not going to go all the way. Ed should have listened to his father's advice. Chickamauga finished out of the money. So did Betty Be Good, and the day became like a shoe slightly too tight, though no one would deny that a too-tight shoe is better than no shoe at all.

By the time of the seventh race, the crowd was more vehement, and mathematics for selecting a potential winner became more complex. Clinton was looking for a long shot. Now Clinton didn't talk so much. He answered his son's questions with grunts and began studying the fluctuating odds. He wanted to see where the smart money was going. Clinton told his son he wouldn't bet until the very last minute. He would put a bundle on the nag that showed the greatest change in the odds.

Then Johnny Le Baron entered the scene. He flicked a cigar ash onto Clinton's racing form, and Clinton had nodded. "Hello, Red."

"This the kid?" Le Baron asked.

Clinton nodded. "My eldest." For his father's sake, Ed acted friendly. The Red Baron, as Johnny Le Baron was called in racing circles, was five foot six with a head of curly red hair. He owned a couple of thoroughbreds and was in tight with some high rollers. Ed had seen him at the inn a number of times. Le Baron befriended Clinton, and Clinton did him a number of small favors, nothing illegal or unsavory, just small things like keeping a parking spot reserved, putting in a good word with the chef, bringing Le Baron trout fresh-caught. As Clinton put it, there were some people worth being on the good side of. Clinton had no real status in the world, so he sought out friends, friends on both sides of the track. Friends gave a man status.

So there stood Johnny Le Baron, dressed to kill, strutting about in a hand-tailored blue suit, with a monogrammed silk handkerchief in his breast pocket. Le Baron pulled out a roll of bills large enough to choke a horse. "Like the track, eh, kid?"

"Yeah. It's great," Ed lied.

"Like father, like son, they say. I went to my first race when I was three months old. My old lady says that I picked the winner by drooling on the program in the right place." Le Baron paused. He peeled off a brand new hundred-dollar bill. "Here, kid, get your old man and me two double scotches, and get a Coke for yourself. Buy us a couple of club sandwiches while you're at it. Get something for yourself too."

"Thanks," Ed said, taking the money. He looked at his father's face for a clue. He couldn't figure anything out.

"Hitting the big ones?" Le Baron asked.

"A few," Clinton said without blinking. "You got anything running?"

"Ran mine early." Le Baron turned to Ed. "What are you waiting for, kid? Didn't I give you enough money?"

Ed went up to the clubhouse and brought back the scotches and the sandwiches. He didn't buy anything for himself. The seventh race had just gotten underway. "Who we got?" Ed asked his old man.

"Nobody," Le Baron replied. He took his change without counting it. The seventh's for suckers. We're saving our wad for the eighth. The eighth is going to be a boat race. I can pick 'em, can't I, Clint?"

"You sure can," Clinton said. There wasn't much enthusiasm in his voice. Ed wished that Le Baron would go away.

"The last time I gave your old man a tip," Le Baron told Ed, "Lo and Behold came in and paid 15 to 1." He turned to Clinton for corroboration.

"You sure can," Clinton repeated, refolding the racing form and swatting the railing with it. Drake's Delight took the seventh by five lengths and paid a paltry $4.20, $3.40, and $2.20. Clinton turned away from Le Baron and took out his faded tan wallet. He counted out two twenties and a ten. Ed was not so much interested in the money being taken out as by the bills that were left behind. His father had at most three or four dollars left.

"Maybe we should go," Ed suggested, taking a sip from his father's scotch. "Mom wants me to mow the lawn."

"After the eighth you hire a gardener," Le Baron said, moving closer to the group. The three of them were standing in the open area in front of the seats. It was that time of day when men and women who had just gotten off work began to straggle in. "Poor stiffs," Le Baron said, waving his hand as if he were showing off his personal property. "Imagine having to work on a day like this. If you know how to use your head, kid," he said to Ed, "you never have to work. You can follow the ponies from one land of sunshine to another." He took out his money clip and slid out another C-note. "This is for Woe-Be-Gone. On the nose." He looked at Clinton. Clinton nodded and handed his son a wad of bills. "The same for your old man. What did I tell you?"

"Woe-Be-Gone," Ed said, as if he were reciting a lesson. "To win."

"The kid's got a head on his shoulders, Clint. When did I ever play anything else but to win?" He took a sandwich from the tray.

"I'll go get the tickets," Ed said.

"What's your rush, kid? There's plenty of time." Le Baron tossed the half-eaten sandwich back. "Garbage."

Ed ran back to the ticket sellers' area. He studied the black man who was chalking up the odds. Woe-Be-Gone was going off at 75 to 1. A gray-haired man with a toothpick in his mouth was leaning against a green post. Ed was standing close enough to see that he was circling Patent Pending. On the board, Patent Pending was the favorite. He circled the printed name over and over as if the repetition implied a special magic. "Durango's Darling," a woman said. On the board Durango's Darling was going off at 12 to 1.

"What?" Ed asked.

"Durango's Darling, honey," the woman said.

"Yeah. Yeah. Thanks." Ed walked away from her. The gentleman with the toothpick stayed put, his yellow stub of a pencil going round and round and round, making a black track on the paper. Odds on Woe-Be-Gone had dropped to 60 to 1. Ed didn't know what to make of it, though in late races more people tended to bet long shots in order to recoup their losses.

Ed studied the C-note. He liked the feeling of holding a hundred and fifty dollars in his hands all at once. It gave him a feeling of power. A man with money like that to throw around could get all the women he wanted.

There were six minutes to post time. The odds on Durango's Darling were holding steady. Patent Pending had fallen to 5 to 1. A horse named Fathom became the new favorite. Ed liked playing the favorites and not the long shots, and he wondered if the Red Baron knew that Clinton was betting only $50.00 to Le Baron's $100.00. That's why the old man gave him the bills all wadded up, so that Le Baron couldn't read the amount. Ed eased the wad of bills into his pocket and watched the black man chalk up the new odds. It was all very pleasant, the way everything changed over and over again.

Ed studied the board. Patent Pending looked better all the time. He crossed to the window where the woman had been and put down two dollars to win on Patent Pending. The odds had dropped to 5 to 1. A man behind Ed bought a win ticket on number 4–Swab the Decks, going off at 11 to 1.

Ed stepped back and refolded his father's money. $48.00 left. Suppose he didn't place the bet at all, he thought. Then when Woe-Be-Gone didn't come in, as it was obvious to Ed that it wouldn't, then nobody would be the wiser, and his old man would be $148.00 to the good–even more if Patent Pending won. Ed could give the money to his mother, and there would be peace at home.

The betting lines had grown longer in the final two minutes to post time, but Ed retreated from them. The black man was working the chalkboard like a gandy dancer. Ed recounted the $148 and neatly folded it, placing it inside a handkerchief and then into his front pocket, with his heart pounding louder than he could imagine. As slowly as possible, he rejoined Le Baron and his father.

"Got the tickets, kid?" Le Baron asked. His face was beet red.

Ed nodded. He turned away to watch the horses being led into the starting gate.

"Good. Hold them for luck."

As the gates slammed behind the horses, the sound rang out louder than usual.

"You all right?" Ed asked his father.

"Yeah," Clinton said. "You? You want anything more to eat?"

"Naah. I'll wait for the race to end."

"Yeah." Clinton wiped the sweat from his forehead. "Wait for the race to end."

The bell rang. Swab the Deck broke first, taking the early lead, followed closely by Durango's Darling, Fathom, and Patent Pending. Woe-Be-Gone was lost with four other horses in the rest of the pack. The crowd was subdued, but as the horses neared the first turn, the noise swelled. Le Baron snatched the pair of binoculars from Clinton's hands. Clinton did not protest. "Give him the bat, you bastard, give him the bat!" Le Baron cried.

Patent Pending made his move, going to the outside, gaining lengths so that as the nine horses neared the final turn, the order was Fathom, Patent Pending, and Durango's Darling. Swab the Deck had fallen way off. On the outside, Woe-Be-Gone was running easily. Bettors pushed toward the railing. Ed was jammed in. There was an empty feeling in the pit of his stomach. "Come on Woe-Be-Gone," Ed's old man shouted. Le Baron gestured with the glasses. "He's getting ready to make his move," Le Baron shouted, "Howeser is going to the bat."

The horses headed into the stretch. Fathom had lost his strength. Durango's Darling was nowhere to be seen. Patent Pending was in front by two lengths, but Woe-Be-Gone was coming on, with Howeser applying the whip. Fathom fell back to fourth. A horse named Claim Digger had moved into third. Woe-Be-Gone second. Ed's old man pounded the railing with his rolled newspaper. Ed couldn't watch. The two horses were neck and neck. "What did I tell you?" Le Baron asked. "All Howeser's got to do is boot the horse home." Ed prayed to himself: No, God, no. I'll do anything. I promise. He clutched the railing to keep from falling into a faint. The horses were running, running, running. He didn't have to look up to know who had won.

To hear Deep-in-Despair MacAdoo tell the rest of the story over a beer in some late-night dive is enough to make a body weep, because there was Ed with $148.00 in his front pocket, and the black man up at the tote board chalking up figures like an adding machine gone berserk. Woe-Be-Gone had paid a cool $138.00 to win on a two-dollar bet.

"Now you know who your friends are," Le Baron said, wiping the binoculars on his sleeve and returning them to Ed's old man.  Ed didn't move from the rail. Perhaps it was a mistake. Perhaps Howeser had fouled somebody coming through. Ed waited for the announcer to take it all back. Patent Pending paid a measly $5.40 to place, $3.60 to show.

Clinton placed his hand upon his son's shoulder. Ed jumped "What's the matter, son? Something bothering you? You look like you've seen a ghost."

"I told you," Le Baron repeated. "Next time come to Johnny Le Baron if you want to go home winners."

"I was just thinking how surprised mom is going to be," Ed said. Oh God, let Howeser commit a foul!

"Yeah, well, forget mom for a while. You and me are going off for the best steak dinner money can buy."

"Sounds good," Ed said weakly. He didn't have to be a whiz at arithmetic to figure out how much he owed Le Baron. He'd have to work full-time for over two years to pay him back, and then some. Ed turned back to the black man chalking figures on the tote board. Clam Digger paid $7.20 to show.

"Where you going, kid?" Le Baron asked.

"Going to cash the tickets." Bluff it out to the very end, Ed figured. Maybe a miracle would happen. Maybe a sudden thunderstorm would come up and he'd be struck by lightning.

"You look sick, son."

"The kid had too much excitement. Hell, Clint, you just earned better than a half year's salary."

"I'm going down to say a few words to Howeser," Le Baron said. "Get the money, kid, and buy yourself a thoroughbred on the way back." Le Baron clapped his hands together and laughed.

Some joke, Ed thought. "What about the ninth race?" he asked. Why don't I just let it all ride?"

"Got a real gambler there, Clinto. A real gambler. Wants to let it all ride."

It was a desperate gambit. "You only live once," Ed said, trying to make it sound nonchalant.

"What has he been drinking?" Le Baron asked. "Don't he know about the race?"

"Go cash the tickets," Clinton said quietly, twisting The Morning Telegraph tightly, "and meet us back here."

Ed walked. He walked from one end of the betting area to the other. His head was spinning. His shirt was soaked through. He could only stall so long; he'd have to tell his father the truth sooner or later. How could be phrase it? Hey, dad, you're really not as rich as you think you are. Hah. Hah. Hah. They'd all have a good laugh. And Le Baron would take out a gun and shoot him right then and there. Better by far to make a run for it. Just keep going and never come back. Return to Tennessee and seek shelter with his grandparents. Ed wandered into the nearest men's room, commandeered the nearest stall, and threw up.

He had cost his father nearly three thousand dollars. How was he going to explain that? That was a year's salary to his old man. At least. What good would the $148.00 do him now? What an idiot he had been! He had no right to stay alive. The inevitable, with a capital I, stuck a catcher's mitt in his puss. He cleaned the toilet as best he could and turned back into the men's room, searching for a proper utensil with which to end his existence. There was a row of mirrors. He could break one of the mirrors and slash his wrists.

He could, but he didn't. It didn't seem fair to him that he should take his life without letting his old man know why. His mother might express some interest in the matter also. He searched his pockets for a pencil, but had none on him. For paper he decided to use the two-dollar win ticket on Patent Pending. In search of a pencil, he retreated from the men's room and returned to the cashiers' windows. The concrete beneath his feet was littered with losing tickets. There was one last chance. His old man had told him that people threw away winning tickets every day, people who didn't pay attention, people who got drunk, or people who didn't understand the difference between Win, Place, and Show.

There it was! At his feet, a winning ticket for Number Three—Woe-Be-Gone! A miracle! Bells rang! Angels hovered in the air! Ed MacAdoo, you are among the chosen. He lunged for the ticket, not caring who saw. God had saved him. Unfortunately, the ticket was for the seventh race. He thought he could make the number change by gripping it tightly. Frantically, he got down on all fours and crawled over the tickets. Turning ticket after ticket over, he managed to find a fifty dollar Win Ticket on number 1 in the Eighth. Then, miracle of miracles, a hundred dollar win ticket on number 7, Swab the Deck. That's what he was doing all right. A half-formed excuse formed in his brain.

He stood up and brushed his blue pants. Swab the Deck. That's right. He'd take the money he had left, run off, and join the Navy.

"What's the matter, son?" Ed turned, his breath going from him. There was his father. "Did you get the money?" Ed's father had washed, combed his hair, and straightened his tie. He looked twenty years younger. "We've been waiting twenty minutes for you. I was beginning to worry. Le Baron thought you had run out on us." Clinton grinned.

"Yeah?"

"Did you get the money?" Clinton repeated. He reached out and brushed the hair away from Ed's eyes.

"Uh...nah."

"Then give me the tickets. I'll get it if you're scared. There's nothing they can do. It's our money." Clinton held his right hand palm up.

Ed made a series of half-hearted, broken gestures before the tears came. "I don't have them."

Clinton's face went white. "What do you mean?"

"I was on my way to get in line when two guys jumped me and took the tickets from me."

Clinton snapped his fingers impatiently. "Don't lie to me, son."

In desperation, Ed held forth the two tickets he had picked up from the floor. Clinton took the tickets and examined them. With disgust, he gave them back to his son. "These aren't the right tickets," he said flatly. "Where are the ones you bought?"

"Those are the ones I bought."

Clinton studied his son's face for a sign that his son was joking.

"I bought the wrong tickets," he wailed.

"On purpose?" Clinton looked like a ghost.

"By accident. The guy gave me the wrong tickets."

"Ed, I don't know what's going on," his father's voice pleaded, "but you found these on the floor."

"I threw them away and found them back. Honest. I'm not lying."

Clinton shook head to toe. "What do you mean you got the wrong tickets?" Because of the crowds, he still hadn't raised his voice. "What are you telling me? Do you know what you're telling me? Did some hop-head give you something?"

"I asked for the number three like you told me, but the ticket seller must have given me the wrong tickets."

"On two different numbers? What am I, Ed, crazy? Is this some kind of a joke? Because if it is, it's not funny. It's got to stop right now. You hear me, young man. You're playing with my sweat and blood."

"No joke, sir. No joke!" He blurted out so loudly that people in the cashier lines turned to stare. His old man grabbed Ed by the elbow and dragged him under the iron-green staircase that led to the upper level. There in the shadows, Ed sobbed out his story and gave his old man the $148.00 wrapped in his handkerchief. Clinton collapsed against the wall as if he were suffering a heart attack. "I'm sorry, I'm sorry, I'm sorry." It was all Ed could say.

"Jesus," Clinton said, the name barely audible. "Jesus! What've you done to me, kid." His hands were on his chest and his face was contorted with pain. "The Red Baron himself gives me a gold-plated ringer and you don't even buy the goddamn ticket because Mom is afraid of not having a piece of meat on the table? Jesus! This is not happening to me, is it? Tell me it all over. Tell me like it's a bad dream. I got a year's salary in my pocket, and my son doesn't have enough brains to buy the goddamn ticket!"

"How did I know the race was fixed?" Ed asked, his words coming in gasps.

"How did you know it was fixed? How do you know anything? You know things because I tell you, that's why. Don't you know nothing? Number three, number three. Fifty dollars to win on number three." With both hands, Clinton struck his son, knocking him back and forth across the neck and shoulders, shoving his head against the bottom of the staircase. Ed made no attempt at resistance, not even raising his arms; his face blotched with crying, until he collapsed onto the floor, drawing his legs up to his chest.

"I'll do anything," Ed bawled. "Anything. I'll earn that money back for you."

"What's there to do?" Clinton roared. "What's there to do? Can you put your hand in your pocket and fish out nine grand like that?" He smashed his right hand against the bottom of the stairwell, bringing it forward, bleeding at the knuckles. People were climbing up and down the stairs, but nobody stopped to look.

Ed sat up, leaning his head on his knees. Clinton took the $148.00 and allowed the bills to flutter about his son's ears. "Take that home to your mother," Clinton said. "Tell her how much you won for her today."

"Let me tell Le Baron," Ed begged.

"Stay put, until I tell you. You're not doing nothing. Don't you think you've done enough already?"

"Give him the $148.00."

Clinton walked away. He was gone a long time, and he didn't come back for his son. Ed huddled under the stairwell and listened to the sounds of the track being locked up. It wasn't until after dark when a black man found him. The janitor told him they wouldn't call the police if he left right away without causing nobody any trouble. They unlocked one of the chain-link gates and shoved him off. Ed, making certain he had the money with him, walked the five miles home.

It was ten-fifteen when Ed reached home. His old man's car was not parked in the driveway. Ed's mother, dressed in her favorite red bathrobe with matching slippers, sat in the front room, waiting.

"Edward?"

Ed crossed in from the hallway. "Did you have fun?" his mother asked, not looking at him.

"Is he home?" Ed asked.

"Did you two have a fight? I hope you two ain't fighting. There's hardly enough peace in this house as it is. Lord knows I pray for peace in this house. It's not too much for a body to ask, is it? Who drove you home?" She did not stir from where she was sitting, merely reached for a flyswatter and batted it listlessly.

"Nobody." Ed took out the $148.00 and spread it on the coffee table. "I walked."

Edwina stared at the bills spread before her and covered her mouth with her hand. When she took her hand down, all she said was, "Lord have mercy. Lord have mercy. What have you brung home?" Allowing the flyswatter to drop, she gathered up the bills and counted them. "One hundred and forty-eight dollars. What is this, Edward? These your father's winnings?"

Exhausted, Ed dropped into the flower-patterned easy chair next to the Philco radio. "Yeah. They're his winnings, all right."

"Lord a mercy." His mother's face broke into a smile. "Clinton never said nothing about winnings when he called."

Ed was pulled in a jerk. "He called? What did he say?"

"Just said some business came up and that he had to go out of town right away."

"Right away?" Ed stood up.

"Sounded strange to me. The way he talked. I figured you and him lost his shirt. He never said nothing about winnings."

"When did he call?"

"I don't know. Sometime in the afternoon. Seems strange that he didn't bring you home first. I don't know. What's a body to think these days?" She recounted the money and folded the bills neatly. "I guess I had better put this away before somebody around here gets more wild notions about betting it away. You hungry? I'll make you a sandwich. I got some good ham this afternoon. Of course some people just think they can come home anytime they please and there will be supper waiting for them."

"I'm not hungry," Ed said. He crossed to the radio.

Without turning the radio on, he fiddled with the dials. His mother turned back into the room and brushed Ed's blond hair away from his eyes. "I guess you brought your father a lot of luck today, honey."

It was four or five days later, when Ed realized that Clinton was never coming home, that deep, deep, deep despair finally set in. Deep-in-Despair MacAdoo. It's some moniker, all right.

# EVERYTHING I KNOW ABOUT LULU

Let me tell you how it was. My folks was living in Paris at the time—not France Paris, but Paris, Tennessee—and it was just an ittie-bittie town then, though we weren't right in the town proper, but we were plunked up on one of those green grass hills that laid off towards the west where Pa hoped he could laze around and nobody'd bother him. It was 1938, and I was all of nine at the time, and my best friend Lulu was eleven. By rights Lulu should have been Girlie's best friend, but Lulu and my sister didn't get along too good. I don't know why. They just didn't. Lulu wasn't all that smart, and she hung out with me a lot, and her and me visited each other across the holler. Some people might call it the hollow, but it was really the holler because people were hollering back and forth across it all the time. Pig-calling and drunk-yelling. On a summer's night it would be awful difficult to get to sleep.

But it was 1938 and the Depression had worn pretty thin on all of us. I remember it all pretty good because that year we didn't even have a house. What we did have was a bed that Ma had set up under a tree. Over our bed was a ramshackle tin roof that Pa had managed to nail across the branches. One roof. One bed. That was all the shelter we had. All five of us—Ma, Pa, Girlie (which was my older sister), and Daniel Boone Dunlap (which is my little brother), and me (which is Betsy)–slept toe to toe. It's stuff like that that can ruin a girl for life. Not that I was ruined, you understand, but Girlie turned out to be pretty sullen in her old age, always bickering and whining, and poor Daniel Boone went in and out of Memphis with something the doctors call schizophrenia.

The reason we had no house was simple. Pa was just too lazy to build one for us. My friend Lulu's folks were hardly no better off than we'en, what with all the folks in The Holler living on turnip greens and grit, but at least Lulu's Pa had the gumption to chop down a few trees and build himself a regular cabin with a front and back porch and all. That's why whenever I could I would go running across the holler with my dress flapping so that I could sleep on her back porch with Coot, the old hound, nuzzling his cold nose at me. Ma and Pa didn't mind none whether I came home or not because it meant one less mouth to feed and more room in the bed to twitch around in. Pa liked all the sleeping space he could get, and there was a stretch in early June when he hardly moved out of bed for two whole weeks. I remember at one point that he took a WPA job, but he only lasted two days, and when he came back, he said it left a terrible bad taste in his mouth.

Most of the time me and Girlie and Daniel Boone traipsed around the holler scavenging bits of food out of people's trash buckets. Daniel couldn't walk good, but he could crawl into places that you could hardly think of. Of course the neighbors were usually pretty kind about giving us kids something, but many of them didn't have much neither. No wonder they was always grumbling against Pa, and saying they was going to do something to him because he had no right not taking care of his family like that. Some of them wondered why Ma wouldn't get up and leave him, but I guess Ma was pretty lazy herself, and besides everybody knows that a woman's got to make do with what she gets married to out of her own free will. Of course I never married so I can't say what I would have done had I been Ma and Ma had been me.

Maybe I should add that it wasn't all that bad as it sounds.

There was some summer nights when the wind blew across our sleeping something soft, and even when it rained, I mean if it weren't a rip-roaring downpour or typhoon, the sound of raindrops pinging on the tin roof could waken in a body all sorts of thoughts, even the body of a girl that ain't yet turned woman. There is lots to be said for living free outside in one's own yard, so I don't want to make it sound no worse than it was.

But, as I said, our neighbors didn't take kindly to Pa's lazing ways and were not all spitting over with joy when we children turned up on their doorsteps with our bellies in our hands, so one fine morning Pa crawls hisself out of bed and steps–crack!–right down onto a pile of sticks that someone had set out in the middle of the night as a warning. Pa hopped around with his foot in his hand but he didn't say much. We knew what he was thinking, because when mountain folk leave a pile of sticks on somebody's land it means that somebody is in for a good licking unless that person shapes up and changes his ways. Pa could see the writing on the wall, but he didn't do much about it. Getting everybody together and lighting out would take more energy than he was willing to give to such a project.

The rest of the morning, Pa lazed about, but the pile of sticks was right under his nose, so his lazing didn't have the same feeling to it that it had before. Around about noon, a big rainstorm broke, and it was a good drenching we all got, what with the wind blowing and all. Finally the sun broke through, and there was the most humdinger rainbow that I had ever seen. Not the itty-bitty type you usually get, but a whole rainbow reaching right down to the both ends of the earth, and you just know that somewhere, sometime, somehow, someone is going to go all the way to the end of it and find a pot of gold sitting there waiting. Daniel Boone and I talked about that all afternoon, and Daniel Boone would have lit right out for it too if I hadn't tied him to a tree with a bit of clothesline. Of course it would have been a good horse laugh on Pa if Daniel Boone came toddling back with a pot of gold swinging under his arm.

Toward dusk Pa was in such a horrible mood, worrying about

that pile of sticks and swearing up a blue streak, that I took my blanket and wandered across the holler to Lulu's place. Our bed was pretty soaked from the rain anyway.

When I climbed up onto the porch of Lulu's cabin, old Coot yawned a kind of greeting at me, and I spread out my blanket and waited. There wasn't all that much to do so waiting took up a lot of time. I guess everybody in Lulu's family had gone off hunting back into the woods or was working the still. Every once in a while the hot air was interrupted by a shotgun going off and then a man's voice a-whooping and a-hollering like it was far away in a dream. Maybe one of Lulu's brothers would bring back a turkey, and we would have a feast, though even I knew that wild turkey was about the toughest creature on earth to hunt, and even if you do kill one, its meat is so stringy it's like chewing on a mess of yoyo cord. Old Coot yawned. Him and me was the same. We both knew that if you couldn't eat and couldn't stop thinking about eating, then the best thing to do is to sleep. But it was too early to sleep. There was a long time in my life when sleep never did come at the right time.

Finally Lulu showed up. She was just walking around the yard in her underwear, and her face was all red and blotched like she had been crying. She sat beside me, the two of us so scrawny that we musta looked like two scarecrows sitting knee to knee.

"See the rainbow this afternoon?" I asked her.

Lulu brushed the blonde hair away from her eyes. "Walked through it," she said. She was acting tough, but I knew different. Usually you'd say something to Lulu, and then you'd wait a long time, and then maybe you'd get a reply or maybe you wouldn't. I could tell from the way that she answered me quick that something had happened.

"You're not supposed to do that, Lulu," I told her.

"I know, but I did anyway." We thought about that for a while. Some people have got to think things through even if they don't have much to think with. "Bubba says that I'm going to change into a boy."

"Bubba should know," I told her. I was really annoyed with Lulu going through the rainbow like that, so I didn't try to soften the blow none. Besides, if her own brother wouldn't do it, why should I? Bubba was one of Lulu's older brothers—she had a mess of 'em. Sometimes when Bubba had stayed down at the still too long, he would put on one of Lulu's dresses and do an imitation of Lulu that was just like her pouting out her cheeks and pushing back her hair. You'd be rolling all over the ground with your sides just aching. I liked Bubba best of all Lulu's brothers because he wasn't dumb. He knew things. I knew things too, but I didn't know how to say them all the time. Of course, it was no dark secret what would happen to a body once it had passed beneath a rainbow. If you were a girl, you would change to a boy. If you were a boy, you'd change to a girl. It was just one of those things that everybody knew about. I had even heard Ma say such a thing herself. Ma had a girlfriend over in Memphis who it happened to, and she had to go down and work in the factory right along with her brothers, lifting and loading. It was enough to give a young girl nightmares.

"How long do you think it's going to take?" Lulu asked me. I could see her eyes all welling up with water, so I looked away. I didn't say nothing. I just shrugged my shoulders.

"Probably takes all night," she said.

"I guess."

"And then I'll wake up and I'll be a boy and that will be that." Actually, it sounded pretty simple once she said it like that. "Stupid rainbow!" she added, standing up and going into the house. I didn't say nothing. I just let my brain stir things around. I watched old Coot scratch his ear with his foot. That's one advantage a hound has over us. Then I thought that maybe Lulu should consider herself lucky that she was changing into a boy and not a hound dog. Especially a hound dog like Coot. Every cloud has a silver lining, my Ma used to say.

I fell back on the blanket and dozed off. It was a real talent I had then—being able to sleep. It was better than staying awake hungry. Anything is better than that, I guess.

I slept like a log, but that was because I was sleeping by myself, and when I awoke, there was a boy standing right by the top of my head. First I sniffed the mud-caked boots and then I saw them; then my eyes moved up the black pants and the black jacket, and across the face partially hidden by a broad scarecrow's hat.

"Bubba?"

"Just me," Lulu answered. She walked back toward her hammock and sat down, her legs dangling off the ground. The moonlight was flooding the porch as if everything around us wanted a share of the great mystery.

"You?" I bolted straight up. I was so young then that sleeping on a mess of boards didn't bother me none, the way it would now. "Has it happened?"

"How do I know?"

"Holy cow! If you don't know, nobody does." I was angry with myself that I had missed the whole thing. It didn't seem fair to me, to be so close to something out of the ordinary and then sleeping through it the way Pa would. But I guess I had Pa's blood in me, and once you get bad blood in you, you've got it for life, unless you go to a conjure man, but we were poor Whites and had no truck with that kind of stuff. Lulu had gone and become a boy, and there I was, stretched out, dead to the world, snoring away like a dumb dog.

I joined Lulu on the hammock and we swung slowly back and forth. "What does it feel like, Lulu," I whispered. I wasn't sure how late it was, but it felt late, and the rest of her family was inside sleeping up a storm, especially Lulu's old lady, who had a barrelful of noise inside of her. I had been sleeping on Lulu's back porch so much it had become a kind of music to me.

"It doesn't feel like nothing because nothing has happened yet." I breathed a sigh of relief. The pains in my stomach were kicking up something awful, but I wasn't about to doze off again.

"No?" I asked. "You certainly look like Bubba to me."

"I just put on his clothes. I figured I had better get used to wearing them."

That made sense to me. Old Coot had abandoned a half-chewed

turkey leg, so I jumped off the hammock and fetched it. There wasn't much meat left on it, but I could suck the marrow out of it. That's what I liked about Lulu's hound. He was just like my Pa. He was too lazy to get up and bury his own bones.

"I'm glad I'm not turning into a boy," I said, "because Daniel Boone's clothes would be much too short for me." Lulu didn't say anything. She just sat there like death warmed over. I didn't want to be mean to her, but I couldn't help myself because she was so dumb, walking through a rainbow like that and ruining everything. I was going go lose my only friend, unless Lulu became my boyfriend, but I knew that wouldn't be the same. To tell the truth, at that time I really wasn't in the mood for a boyfriend.

"Anything happening?" I asked.

Lulu placed her hand down the front of Bubba's pants and touched herself.

"Can I look?" I asked.

Lulu stood up, untied the piece of rope, and let Bubba's pants drop to her ankles. I looked, but she didn't have a thing like Bubba's. I guess nothing was happening. It makes you wonder sometimes why everything in life takes so long to happen.

"You got a name picked out?" I asked her.

Lulu pulled Bubba's pants back up and climbed back onto the hammock. "Lulu's not much of a boy's name, and Bubba and Scottie are already taken."

Lulu thought about that for a while, rubbing her hand over the front of her body like she was trying to remember it. "Tom," she said at last. "Tom. I'm going to call myself Tom. Like in Tom Mix."

"Tom." I repeated the name about twenty times in order to get used to saying it. I walked over to the hammock and stared at Lulu. She was pretty much the same, but I had to admit that she looked pretty puny in the hammock. No matter how big someone looks, they always look pretty puny when they lie down. "Hey, Lulu," I whispered.

"What?"

"Do you think there's the same number of boys in the world as there are girls?"

"What?"

"Do you think there's the same numbers of boys in the world as there are girls? I mean, there would have to be, wouldn't there? Otherwise some boy would have a girl, and some girl wouldn't have a boy. That makes sense, doesn't it?"

"I guess," Lulu said with a lot of tiredness in her voice.

"Well, then, that means if someone changes into a boy, then someone else somewhere else has got to change into a girl just to keep it even. You know what I mean?"

Lulu didn't, but she said she did. I don't know why I even bothered to ask her in the first place. We just sat quiet and thought about it for a while. Out in the woods, by a stand of pine, I swore the shadows were changing shapes, like sometimes they were trees and sometimes animals–deer with their heads down.

"Mattie?"

I jumped. My real name is Betsy, but I sometimes let Lulu call me Mattie. I don't know why, I just do. To tell the truth, I'm really not fond of Betsy because Betsy is the name of Pa's ma, and I'm not very fond of her neither.

"I'm scared," Lulu wailed, and I went over to her. There was a big rip in her wailing where my name got through.

"Hey, Lulu, what's going on?" I whispered. I held out my hand to her, and she grabbed it, squeezing it like she was trying to keep the blood from flowing through it. "Is it happening?"

She nodded. "Hold me, Mattie," she cried. "Hold me."

"O.K., Tom," I said, and I climbed onto the hammock and held her. I pressed my body on her, and she was very quiet, and both of us finally drifted off to sleep where nobody could ever touch us or would want to.

●　●　●

"Hey!"

"Huh?"

"Git!"

"Huh?"

I was yanked like a fish, a big hand hauling me off the hammock until my heart was in my mouth and my body quivering all over, and there was Lulu's Pa  hovering all over me in the early morning sunlight, holding me in the air, then setting me down with a thud so that my knees touched first and then my head banged against one of my knees. Lulu's Pa was a giant of a man with hardly a tooth in his mouth, and his skin all wrinkled like an old carpetbag, and Lulu, crying, was in the hammock trying to pull Bubba's pants back up, and old Coot was setting up a howl, and I was reaching for something to steady myself, looking for my blanket because I couldn't go home without it.

"What in Hell's damnation has got into you two, sleeping like that," and Lulu didn't say anything but just kept crying. "Git!" her Pa shouted to me, standing there in the bottom half of these dirty long-johns and batting Bubba's black hat at me like I was some kind of insect to be swatted away. I put my hand up to the sun and to the hat, but it didn't do no good because Lulu's Pa was fit to be tied.

"Like what?" I asked him as soon as I could make words.

"Shut your mouth. Just git! I don't want to see you hanging around here again." Lulu jumped up and ran inside the cabin, so I couldn't figure if she had changed to Tom or not.

I was crying too. "I didn't mean nothing," I said.

"Just git, before I tan your hide something good for you. Your whole damn family is no damn good." Lulu's Pa grabbed the blanket away from my outstretched hand and tossed it at me with such force that it almost knocked me off balance, but I held on to it and ran, not hardly awake, not looking back, ran all the way across the holler, wondering what I had done, that maybe he didn't know that Lulu was changing into one of his sons. Or maybe he did know and he was blaming me for something that was none of my fault. I ran and

I ran, with old Coot tagging at me like he was my own hound and didn't belong to the Klemms at all. So there I was struggling with the blanket and the day and a dog that wasn't even mine and Lulu changing into something that she wasn't even meant to be.

I didn't stop running and old Coot didn't stop barking until I made the ditch, and then I climbed it slowly, up the side of the hill that led into the yard behind the trash pile. I looked around and there was Girlie sitting all by herself in the middle of the bed. Her foot was propped up on the bed railing and she was painting her toe-nails, using one of Ma's old polish bottles. Ma would have tanned her good if she had seen it, but Ma, Pa, and Daniel Boone was nowhere to be seen.

"What are you and old Coot yelping about?" she asked, but she didn't even look up from what she was doing. I guess she didn't care all that much, but I didn't blame her none.

I joined her by sitting down on the edge of the molding mattress and clutched my blanket to my chest. "Nothing," I told her. Anyway it was none of her business. My dress and underpants were all wet and sticky from the run, and I just wanted to throw myself into some water something bad. "Where is everybody?" I asked.

"Gone."

"Gone? Where?"

"Ma said for us to wait here and she'll come fetch us. I was just waiting for you to get back."

Girlie had really pretty feet, long and pointed, which I had never noticed before, but there they were, all propped up on the bedstead with the sunlight upon them. "What happened?" I asked.

Girlie worked the red over her big toe. "Remember that pile of switches? Some of the men-folk from the holler drove up here last night. They got hold of Pa, dragged him right out of bed, put him over the hood of the car, and whipped him something terrible."

"Really?"

"Cross my heart and hope to die." Girlie was always crossing her heart and hoping to die, but she never did. "And that's not all. You knowed what else they done? They made Pa put on a woman's dress, because they said that since he was acting like a lazy woman he ought to dress like one."

"What?"

"What? I just told you what. Now will you stop fidgeting while I'm trying to get this nail polish on?"

"They made Pa wear a dress? Whose dress was it?"

"How do I know?" Girlie was disgusted with me. "Besides, what difference can it make?"

"Did you recognize any of the men?"

"They had masks on, but I guess we recognized them all. It certainly weren't no strangers that don it."

"Well, they warned him," I said, sighing.  I couldn't get over it, the two biggest events in my life and I had missed both of them. It didn't seem right to me. "So where is everybody?" I asked. Not that I cared. It was kinda nice just me and my sister alone.

"They drove Pa around to show the women what he looked like in a dress."

"He's going to be hopping mad," I said. I didn't want to be around when he got back.

"And black and blue," Girlie added.

"You think he's going to come back?"

Girlie shrugged. "You know Pa."

"I guess."

I had never thought about how much Girlie and I looked like one another. I guess that was one of the pleasures in having a sister. You had a living mirror to look into.

"Thanks for waiting for me," I said, watching how carefully she worked the polish around.

"Anytime." She didn't mean it, but I forgave her. I sat back on the bed and told her everything I knew.

# MOMMA WENT AND BOUGHT
# A NEW PAIR OF SHOES

Momma went and bought a new pair of shoes. I knew what that meant. New shoes meant trouble. New shoes always meant trouble. Old shoes meant that you were comfortable in your old life. New shoes meant that a change was coming. The change was that Momma was planning to get married again, and if Momma's fourth marriage was going to be anything like the other three, then both of us were going to be spinning our wheels on a deep and muddy track.

It was 1953, and I was all of thirteen at the time, thirteen going on fourteen, and I was Momma's only daughter, and so I was trying to be protective of her because I didn't want to see her crying no more. Momma would get on these crying jags and stay in bed for two or three weeks at a time. It could get pretty depressing, I can tell you that, and I had my own problems to take care of. Thirteen going on fourteen is not the best age in the world. It's probably the worst age of all for a girl, especially a girl who has a mother who is not all that tightly wrapped, a mother who looks at marriage much the same way that Mae West looks at a grape.

Momma was a good-looker, though, with lots of red hair, and a hourglass figure, with the sand in the right places. She was nearing thirty-nine, though—"Jack Benny's age," she said—and so I guess she was feeling loneliness was giving her the once-over once too often, and she was spending a lot of money making long-distance phone calls to old boyfriends, and even an ex-husband or two. When those long-distance blues get to you, it's time to sing another tune. So when Donnie "The Duck" MacGuire, journeyman third baseman for our one-and-only Charlotte Whips, turns up on our doorstep, carrying flowers and candy and pitching the woo like the woo was a good old-fashioned spitball, well Momma starts losing her grip on reality and starts saying "Yes" all over the place. Next thing I know, Momma's got a new pair of shoes, and I'm destined to play step-daughter to a .249 lifetime batting average. It's nothing to do handstands over, I can tell you that.

Not that I have anything against Donnie "The Duck." Donnie's a fine young man. Yessiree. He's blond, thin as a rail, and a good twelve years younger than my momma. I guess he's what everybody down home calls "a nice guy." He doesn't know much, but he laughs a lot. That should give you something to think about. After all, what can a .249 hitter have to laugh about? Your career is on the line every time you come up to bat. I don't want to give you the impression that Donnie "The Duck" is a moron or anything like that. He's just good-natured, that's all. He'd give you the shirt off his back; but, of course, if you see the shirts he wears, you won't be all that excited to get one. As I have said more than once, Donnie "The Duck" is good-natured, and Momma can wrap him around her little finger and still have room for Joe DiMaggio and Ted Williams and Stan Musial besides.

I could have wrapped Donnie "The Duck" around my little finger, too—that is, if I had wanted to—and so I had to be careful how I acted. I knew that if Donnie "The Duck" started giving me presents or had started to show too much interest, Momma would have gotten awfully jealous, and that kind of trouble a daughter can live without. Not that Donnie "The Duck" ever brought me a great gift. An autographed photo of the entire Charlotte Whips, including the manager, the coaches, and the bat-boy—all of them sitting down on the ground like a human watermelon patch—was never, in my book, going to compete with a diamond as big as the Ritz.

One day such thoughts reminded me to ask Momma why she wasn't sporting a diamond on the fourth finger of her left hand. The question didn't faze Momma. Some days it takes a stick of dynamite to get her going.

"Donnie's going to get me a diamond, Lulu," she said, not blinking an eye. Momma had a way of plucking her eyebrows that reminded me of a fingernail scratching down a blackboard. "Don't you pay the diamond situation no mind. Your momma's going to be sporting a diamond as big as anybody in this country ever seen."

"I bet," I said, not really betting. A man who gives away autographed pictures of the Charlotte Whips is no big spender in my book.

"Mind your manners, Lulu," Momma said sharply, plucking at her left eyebrow. "A .249 hitter has more important things to worry about than buying a woman like me a diamond. I've had diamonds before. Now I want something more lasting. You deserve it. And I deserve it. A good-natured man makes up for a lot of diamonds."

I bet, I thought, but I didn't say a thing. I shut myself up like a pregnant oyster. And that's the way things stood until one Thursday afternoon, when I came home from Jefferson Davis High School and found Donnie "The Duck" sitting in our living room. He looked like he had been hit by a truck, and then the truck backed up, just to make sure.

"Hiya, Donnie," I said, trying to act casual. I had just gone through cheerleading practice, and so I was pretty bushed myself.

Donnie didn't flash no goofy grin the way he usually did. He screwed up his face like he was fighting back tears. "Your momma tore up the wedding license," he said. That's all he said. "Your momma tore up our wedding license."

"Why did she do a stupid thing like that?" I asked.

"I guess she doesn't want to marry me," Donnie said. He sounded like he had struck out with the bases loaded. "It took us awhile to get that license. We had to have blood tests and everything.

Even went to the wrong window first. The man thought we were getting a hunting license."

I didn't want to hear no more of that. I stomped into the bedroom and found Momma sprawled out on the bed. She was fully dressed. Even had her purple hat on with the veil, and she was just wailing and wailing. I had a sudden longing to run back to school and stuff a dead chicken into somebody's locker.

"So you tore up the wedding license?" I asked. It sounded like a good conversation opener to me.

Momma sat up and wiped her eyes. I found some wadded-up tissue for her to blow her nose in. "We were just driving back from the license bureau, and we started arguing about what kind of a wedding to have, and I got so mad, I just took the license and tore the whole thing up."

"You were just making confetti early," I said. It didn't cheer her up none.

"I didn't mean to tear it up," Momma wailed.

"It's only a wedding license," I said, but then I remembered that Momma was a lot older than me.

I walked back out into the living room, where Donnie "The Duck" was practicing to be an undertaker. "She didn't mean to tear up the wedding license," I said. It didn't sound so good coming from me, but I figured someone had to say it.

Donnie's face lit up. "She didn't?"

"If I was you," I told him, "I'd just march right in there and patch things up. You can always buy another license."

"It's two dollars," Donnie said. I shrugged my shoulders and went into the kitchen to make myself a peanut-butter-and-jelly sandwich. Whenever I get depressed, I make myself a peanut-butter-and-jelly sandwich. Then I poured out a big glass of milk. I did it all in a very casual manner. My friends at school would have been real proud of me. Donnie went into Momma's room, and there was a lot of talking back and forth, and when they finally came out, with Donnie's arm around Momma's shoulder, I could see that everything was all right. I guess I had figured that Momma's getting married wouldn't do me no harm, especially with Donnie bringing home a lot of his baseball-playing friends.

Momma tugged at her skirt. "You run over to Grandma's and wait for us there," she said.

"What for?" I asked in my super-casual manner.

"Because, young lady, Donnie and I have to go down to the license bureau and get another license, and I don't want you to stay here all by yourself."

"This time we're going to get a license written on steel so your Momma can't tear it," Donnie "The Duck" said. He let loose a guffaw and then they were out the door, Tweedledum and Tweedledee. Poor Momma, I thought.

I walked over to Grandma Walsh's, and along about six-thirty, quarter-to-seven, Donnie's moth-eaten wagon pulls up and out steps the two lovebirds as if nothing at all had happened. Momma tugged at her skirt, and Donnie punched his hat around before putting it back on top of his head. His hair was so thin and fine that at a distance he looked bald.

Grandma Walsh, who was all of 83 at the time, with skin like leather and a tongue to match, was fit to be tied. Her own daughter hadn't told her about getting married again, and that wasn't the worst of it. The worst of it, from Momma's point of view, was that Grandma wasn't all that fond of Donnie "The Duck." She always called him "That fool!" It's little things like that put a damper on family relations.

"Well, you went and done it this time, Miriam, didn't you?" Grandma said, leaning forward in her rocker, her arms folded tight across her stomach like she had a bellyache. When Donnie climbed up the steps, Grandma started moving that rocker like it was a tank. She stuck out her tongue, but Donnie had been through it all before. He took it in stride.

"Good afternoon," he said, tipping his hat. He tossed me a wink, which was his way of saying that I had done good work a few hours before, getting him and Momma back together again.

"It's not afternoon. It's evening," Grandma said.

"You're right about that, Mrs. Walsh." Donnie "The Duck" sunk into the second rocker and pounded his right fist into his left palm. "I feel so good I thought I'd take you all out to eat this evening." Two months before, Donnie had called Momma's momma "Grannie." We never did hear the end of that one.

"Why don't you get a job like a normal person?" Grandma asked. She had gotten Donnie into her sights, and she wasn't going to let up.

"Oh Momma," Momma wailed.

"Why don't you come down to the park and see me play sometime?" Donnie asked, grinning ear to ear.

Grandma raised her head and sniffed the air. "I'd rather go to a funeral home and watch the bodies rot."

That remark broke Donnie "The Duck" all to pieces, and he was almost falling out of his chair.

"Fool!" Grandma spat.

What Donnie "The Duck" didn't understand about Grandma was (and I know it doesn't make any sense to say it, but it is God's own truth) that she really didn't like people to laugh at her jokes. Grandma would say the weirdest things sometimes, but if you laughed, she would look at you as if you had thrown up in church.

Momma paced back and forth on the porch, clutching the brand new marriage license for all it was worth. I could tell that Momma was worried. She was biting her lower lip and looking daggers at Donnie.

"You two hitched or not, Miriam?" Grandma asked. I always like to listen to my momma getting chewed out by her own momma. It did my heart good.

"We just got the license this afternoon, Momma," my momma said. "We ain't had time to get married yet."

Donnie came up for air. "Hey, Miriam, did you hear what your momma said about going down to the funeral home and watch the bodies rot?" he asked. For an answer, Momma kicked him in the shins.

Donnie clutched his leg. "Auuugh. What was that for?"

"Nothing," Momma said. "Nothing at all."

Grandma held out her bony hand. The back of it was all covered with brown spots—liver spots were what Grandma called them. "Can I see your license, Miriam?"

Momma raised a well-plucked eyebrow. "What for, Momma? It's just like any other marriage license."

"I know, child, but I ain't seen one in a good long while."

Momma sighed and gave the piece of paper to me. I passed it on to Grandma. Donnie followed its progress like we were moving gold. Grandma took the license and pretended to read it. Donnie rocked back and forth, smirking. "Well, Mrs. Walsh, maybe you and I should bury the hatchet," he said.

But Grandma just sat there rocking, tearing the license up, tearing it into a thousand pieces.

"Momma!" my momma cried, but she was too late. Donnie "The Duck's" jaw dropped all the way to his knees. He couldn't believe he was seeing what he was seeing. Momma was down on her knees, trying to gather up the pieces. Tears streamed down her face. Even if she hadn't been my momma, I would have felt sorry for her. I tried to help Momma, but we were only getting in each other's way. Donnie didn't move. He didn't do nothing. He didn't say nothing. He just sat there as if he had swallowed a horse.

"Oh God!" Donnie groaned.

"Don't you curse on my front porch," Grandma said.

"Momma? Why did you tear up my marriage license?" my momma asked.

Grandma just kept at her rocking, working at it like it was her only profession. "I don't know what came over me, Miriam. I just couldn't help myself. That's how it is when you get old. Things come over you, and you just can't help yourself."

"Oh God!" Donnie groaned again.

"I told you before, Mr. Big-League Baseball Player, I won't have no more cursing on my front porch." Grandma tugged at her gray sweater and reached for her cane. Momma backed off, thinking that any minute Grandma might start swinging. With her cane, Grandma was a good .300 hitter. "Besides, child, it's no big thing to bother your head about. You can always get another license."

"Another one?" Donnie asked, raising his head out of his hands. "Another one? I already got two."

"See, Miriam? He says he got two. Who else is he planning to marry?"

Momma stopped picking up the pieces. Sometimes the pieces of things don't do anybody any good.

As you might have guessed, the next morning found the three of us—Donnie, me, and Momma—bright and early at the Marriage License Bureau, a dark cubbyhole of an office set on the third floor of City Hall. Mrs. W. Dunnagin, a pouty-faced woman who wore her hair in a bun and resembled a pigeon, didn't look too thrilled about seeing Donnie again. I knew it was Mrs. W. Dunnagin because that's what the little wooden block on her counter said.

Mrs. Dunnagin stood behind a little half-door-like affair and tapped her pencil against the counter top. "I think I have seen you two before, haven't I?"

Donnie "The Duck" studied the tops of his shoes. They were pretty beat up and in need of a good polishing. I guess he was waiting for his wedding day before getting them shined—that is, if there ever was going to be any wedding day. I studied the electric fan over my head. For some reason, Mrs. Dunnagin reminded me of two-week-old milk.

Momma jabbed Donnie in the shoulder. She wasn't in a good mood because she hadn't gotten much sleep the night before. "The woman's talking to you, Donnie."

Donnie nodded. He knew the woman was talking to him. To him and to nobody else. He cleared his throat. "Well, ma'am, you see, we had a little accident."

"Speak up. I can't hear you," Mrs. Dunnagin said.

"The woman can't hear what you're saying," Momma told Donnie. I kept looking at the fan and wishing I was dead. Standing right behind us were two teenagers. They looked as if they were in an awful hurry to get married. From what I had seen of marriage, I couldn't understand why anyone would want to go to the bother.

"We had a little accident," Donnie said.

"Accident? What do you mean by accident?" Mrs. Dunnagin demanded.

"That's what I'm trying to tell you, ma'am," Donnie said, his eyes not lifting from the tops of his shoes.

"You don't have to sass me, young man."

"I wasn't trying to sass you, ma'am. I was just trying to tell you."

"For God's sakes, Donnie, tell her," Momma said.

Mrs. Dunnagin folded her hands and placed them out in front of her as if she was praying. "I have better things to do than to issue you the same marriage license over and over again."

"I know, ma'am. I really do."

"Do you?"

"I really do."

"Ma'am," the pimply-faced boy behind me said.

Mrs. Dunnagin waved him away. "Be with you in a minute. Marriage lasts a lifetime. It can wait a few minutes."

"My dog chewed it up," Donnie said.

"What?"

"The marriage license? My dog chewed it up."

"That's what I thought you said."

"So if you could just issue us another license, we'll be on our way. We won't bother you no more."

Donnie "The Duck" looked so pathetic that I guess he touched a soft spot in Mrs. Dunnagin's pouty little heart. "All right. For another two dollars, I'll issue you another license. But this had better be the last one."

"Yes, ma'am."

"But you'll have to wait because I'm going to have to take care of these young'uns first." She waved the pimply-faced boy and his pregnant girlfriend to the head of the line. I went out into the hallway to find the water cooler. After about thirty minutes, Donnie and Momma came out, and we went down to Donnie's car.

"Why don't we get married today before we lose this thing," Donnie suggested. It was the first smart thing I had heard him say in a long time.

"Because I want my momma to be there when I get married, that's why," my momma said. She opened the glove compartment in Donnie's car and tucked the marriage license in there for safe-keeping, sliding it under a map of North Carolina. "Besides, you have a game this afternoon with the Canton Tigers. Or have you forgotten that?"

"No, Miriam, I haven't forgotten," Donnie said, driving away like he had just robbed a bank. "But your momma's not going to come to our wedding. She doesn't like me."

"She'll come," Momma said. "Momma always says she won't come, but she always comes. It's kind of a good luck charm." There was a lot I could have said about that, but I didn't. Donnie took us home and went off to the game. Even I knew that .249 hitters don't forget when they have games to play.

I was in the middle of the Civil War when the phone rang. Momma talked for a few minutes, and then she started to cry and to curse up a storm, which really wasn't like Momma at all. Then she hung up. Then she sat down and started to laugh. Soon the laughing and the crying were all mixed in together. Finally she said, "Donnie's had his car stolen."

"Stolen?" I wasn't thinking about the car.

"He came out to the parking lot after the game, and the car wasn't there." Momma wasn't thinking about the car either.

"Maybe one of his friends borrowed it," I suggested. All of a sudden I understood what my teacher had said about the start of the Civil War. I don't know why I understood it. I just did.

"He's reported it as stolen." Momma's eyes were beginning to get puffy.

"Nobody would want that old heap," I said. "If people are

going to steal cars, why don't they steal Cadillacs and leave the old ones alone."

"I shouldn't have put the license in the glove compartment," Momma said.

I agreed, but couldn't say I agreed. In our minds, it had become "The License." I pretended that I was studying my history lesson, but it was no use. "Who won the game?" I asked as casually as I could.

"I didn't ask," Momma said. "I didn't ask."

Momma didn't relish going back down to City Hall and trying to get a license– "The License"–from Mrs. Dunnagin, and nobody could blame her; but Donnie "The Duck" wasn't going to go in there alone, and nobody could blame him either. It wasn't his fault that the car was stolen. If he said that once, he said it a thousand times. Donnie asked if I would go with him, and I reluctantly said yes. I figured it was in Momma's best interest, and so I went.

"What now?" Mrs. Dunnagin screamed when she saw Donnie and me coming through the door. The stack of files she was carrying fell to her feet. "You want to marry her too, I suppose," she said with a great chill. She meant me.

"I don't want to marry her," Donnie said. He meant me. "I want to marry her mother." Before coming into the office, I had given Donnie a little pep talk, warning him to be more assertive.

"So go marry her," Mrs. Dunnagin said. "That's across the hall, not here."

Panic set in. "But I need another license," Donnie blurted out. "My car was stolen."

Mrs. Dunnagin took three steps back as if someone had punched her. "You what?"

"His car was stolen," I said.

Mrs. Dunnagin breathed a sigh of relief. "Oh, so you're talking about a driver's license this time."

"No, ma'am, a marriage license."

Mrs. Dunnagin raised an eyebrow. "Another one?"

"It was in the glove compartment of the car," I said.

"And the car was stolen," Donnie added.

"But I've given you three licenses already," Mrs. Dunnagin said. Even I could sense the despair in her voice. She wasn't casual about it at all.

"My car was stolen," Donnie repeated. "It wasn't my fault."

"You shouldn't have kept it in the car," she said. "It was the third one I gave you. You shouldn't have kept it in your car."

"I couldn't agree with you more, ma'am." Donnie said. "But I didn't know that my car would be stolen."

Mrs. Dunnagin frowned. Donnie "The Duck" took out a twenty-dollar bill and held it limply in his hand. He wasn't quite sure what to do with it. I took Donnie's elbow and pushed his arm forward.

"What's all this about?" Mrs. Dunnagin asked.

"For another license, ma'am." Donnie said.

Mrs. Dunnagin drew herself back. "Are you trying to bribe a city official?" she asked with great indignation.

Donnie drew his arm back. "Oh, no, ma'am."

Mrs. Dunnagin didn't pick up the folders she had dropped. She stepped over them and walked behind the counter. She adjusted her nameplate. "I'll tell you what," she said at last. "This is it. You lose this one, I suggest you move to another county. I don't want you to come back in here again. You understand?"

"Yes, ma'am," Donnie said, shifting his weight from one foot to the other. "It's no joke, ma'am. I didn't think my car would be stolen." He was so sincere, no one could doubt him. Mrs. Dunnagin took out an old pen and began to write.

"Maybe you could give me two, just in case?"

Mrs. Dunnagin glanced up from her writing. From the expression in her eyes, no reply was needed.

"Yeah. Well, one would be plenty," Donnie agreed. I studied the fan over my head. It hadn't changed a bit since our last visit.

Outside the building, Donnie offered me the license, but there was no way on God's earth I was going to be responsible for it. I would have preferred to take a job guarding Fort Knox.

"Just take it to your momma," Donnie "The Duck" pleaded.

"You take it to her," I said.

"But I've got to go to the ballpark."

"I don't care. I'm not taking it," I said. He stood with me until the bus came. I got on it and waved good-bye. As I said, I was fond of Donnie. And if he made Momma happy, so much the better for me.

That afternoon, the Charlotte Whips trounced the Canton Tigers 12 to 3. The players were all in a high mood, and some of them went down to Davey Jones's Locker for a few beers. About six hours later, I heard this tapping on my bedroom window. I was up late studying for my history test, and when I heard the tapping, I got scared. But it was only Donnie "The Duck."

"What are you doing?" I asked him, opening the window slightly. I was afraid that maybe he was going to start something with me, that maybe the woman at the license bureau had put ideas into his head. Anyway, it was easy to see that Donnie had been drinking. A lot.

"I've come to say good-bye," Donnie said.

"What do you mean good-bye? Are you and Momma going somewhere?"

"I don't have no license," Donnie said.

"What do you mean, you don't have no license? You and I just got a new one this morning."

"I lost it in the bar."

"Well, go back to the bar and get it. I won't tell Momma. Just go get it." I was beginning to feel sick to my stomach.

"I can't," Donnie moaned.

"Why not?"

"'The Moose' tossed it down the toilet."

"'The Moose'?" I asked.

"Yeah, 'The Moose.' John Berger. That's what he's called: 'The Moose.'"

"Tossed it down the toilet!"

"We were just having a little fun, and when I told them about my marriage license being stolen, they started fooling around, and 'The Moose' grabbed it out of my hands and ran to the men's room and flushed it down the toilet. He thought it was pretty funny. I didn't think it was funny."

"What are you going to do?" I asked.

"I don't know," he said. He looked so sad, so defeated, I felt I should have taken him in my arms and cradled him on my chest. But I didn't. I slammed the window down and turned off the lights. I cried myself to sleep.

Two days later, Momma bought herself a new pair of shoes. Blue satin pumps. They were quite handsome and very expensive. We no longer talked about her marrying Donnie "The Duck." But at least the new shoes made her feel better.

# MUST I WEEP FOR THE DANCING BEAR?

At first I thought it was some kind of a hoax, but then I had never seen anything like it before, so I figured it was worth a few dollars to see what was going on. When I was little I had been to a state fair, but I was too young to remember anything except that it rained a lot. I had never really seen a traveling tent show before, though, and what really caught my eye was the side show with all the drawings outside, so I kept walking back and forth in front of the pictures—an Indian in a turban swallowing fire, a sword swallower, an armless-legless wonder, a magician producing cards out of the air. I had never seen such stuff before, and neither had Gerry. Gerry was my girl then, and that's why I remember it so vividly.

On both sides of the sideshow tent were long blue trailers, and in the one I almost went into there was a picture of Namu, the baby whale. For a quarter, you could go inside and walk around the glass enclosure and could look down on the miracle of miracles, wonder of wonders, quintessence of the ocean, or some such thing. My friends said that the whale was really made out of plaster or papier-mache', but that they weren't sure because the glass was difficult to see through and because the guy out front kept rushing the people through, as if he were afraid of them hurting the whale. Just standing out front by the sign, I heard him tell one of my friends, "Hey look, two bits don't entitle you to rent the trailer for the night. I ain't running no motel for you and your date." Anyway, I don't know whether it was a real baby whale or not. That's just what I heard because, as I said, I didn't go in myself. I was saving my money for better things.

On the other side of the tent, the other trailer showed a picture of the world's largest boa constricter, and one of the posters showed the snake devouring a whole baby elephant. It was frightening to look at, for I was only sixteen at the time, and the whole thing seemed incredible. At the bottom of the poster there had been some writing, but part of it was torn away–probably because the poster had been used so much. Maybe if I had read the writing, I would have believed it, but it didn't seem to me that any snake could eat anything so big. Still there was that picture staring me in the face. Another poster showed the snake devouring a whole pig, and that seemed a little more reasonable to me. I would have gone in, but I didn't have enough money.

While I was waiting for Gerry to come, two Negro kids came up to ask me for a quarter.

"Hey, mistah, how about a quarter so me and my friend can see the bowaconstrikter?"

"So who are you?"

"Boston Blackie."

"What's your friend's name?"

"Jackie Robinson."

"You're a real smart aleck, aren't you?" I said. I looked at Boston Blackie. He couldn't have been more than seven or eight years old. Both he and his friend didn't have anything on except some shorts made of blue jeans cut in half.

"No I ain't. Honest. That's his name," the kid named Boston Blackie said. He wiped his nose with his hand.

"What's your friend going to do while you see the snake. You can't both see it for a quarter."

"So give us two quarters."

"I ain't got two quarters."

"Sure you do. All you white folks got lots of quarters."

"Some do, some don't. I don't. Go pick on someone else."

"What are you? Some kid of poor white trash?"

The boy named Jackie stood back and let Blackie do all the talking. "Yeah, that's what you is all right."

"Look," I said, "take your friend and find someone else to pick on. I was just standing here not bothering anyone."

"Jackie ain't got no father. That's why he ain't got no money for the circus."

"And what's your excuse?"

"Man, you're really nosy. That's what you are."

Out of the corner of my eye, I could see Gerry and Tom Hendrix walking across the field. Tom was a few years older than me and an all-right sort of guy. I guessed he and Gerry had run into each other and happened to be walking in the same direction, because, halfway toward the trailer, Tom went off toward the candy stand. It wasn't that I was jealous or anything. It was just that Tom was a few years older than me and Gerry, and he was pretty good looking. So was Gerry, for that matter, especially in her black shorts and her pink blouse. Usually she let her hair hang free, but that day she had it tied up in back.

"Who's that? Your girl, mistah?" Jackie said. He just looked at me dumbly. He didn't say much of anything.

"Are you his girl?" Boston Blackie asked. Gerry stopped beside me, but didn't answer.

"If you are," he said, "you sure got a cheapskate for a friend. He won't even give me a quarter for the snake."

With her bare feet, Gerry drew some lines in the sand. She hated wearing shoes. "Why don't you give him a quarter for the snake?"

"Because it's a fake, that's why."

"How do you know it's a fake?" Boston Blackie asked.

"What's the matter with you?" I said to Gerry.

"How do you know it's a fake?" Boston Blackie repeated.

"Look, go bother someone else," I said.

"Nothing's the matter," Gerry answered. "I'm all right now.

Why don't we go see the snake?"

"I thought you were afraid of snakes."

"Give us a quarter and we'll go away," Boston Blackie said.

"It doesn't make a difference. Maybe you'll enjoy it."

"But I only have enough money for the sideshow and the main tent."

"Man, you're the cheapest thing I've ever seen," said Boston Blackie. "You wouldn't give the whooping cough away." He took Jackie by the arm, and they went off toward Namu, the baby whale.

"I don't know why those kids don't try to water the elephants or something," I said. "Every time I read about the circus, some kid is always carrying water to the elephants to get inside."

"There don't seem to be that many elephants with this show," Gerry said. She yawned and put her hand to her mouth. "God, I'm tired."

"I guess it's no Barnum and Bailey."

"We ought to do something," Gerry said.

I put my arm on Gerry's shoulder, and we walked over to the entrance of the small tent. There was a wooden platform out front, and the ticket salesman reminded everybody that the main show didn't begin until three-thirty.

"What did Tom have to say," I asked.

"Nothing. He just walked me over. I guess he's going to meet someone here. He says he met one of the girls in the show."

"I bet he has," I said.

"So what do you have against Tom Hendrix?"

"Nothing," I said.

"It sounds like it."

A girl walked through one of the flaps of the tent and climbed up to the wooden platform. "Step right up, folks, step right up. This is Eva, Little Eva with the Sinful Eyes," the man with the microphone said. A few farmers, who had probably snuck away without their wives, began to straggle over, and even a few women stopped to look. I don't care what the man with the microphone said, Little Eva didn't look little to me. She was in her twenties then, at least a few years older than me, and she had a well-developed chest. She was dressed like an Arab dancing girl, with a green veil and all. If you've ever seen a movie about a harem, you know what I mean. As soon as Little Eva reached the platform, the man with the microphone started some music from a portable record player, and Eva began to sway her hips.  Another girl, who the barker called Delilah, also came up to the stage, but she was dressed in blue. Her costume was so thin that I could almost see through it, but I didn't want Gerry to know how excited I was getting. "Crowd in close," the barker said, "so you can see all you can. But remember, folks, this is just a small, a very small, sample of what you're going to see on the inside. If you think that these costumes are skimpy, you should see what the other girls are wearing."

While the man was talking, a third girl came up. She carried a snake which she wound all around her body. The girls danced for a few minutes, and then the man turned off the record player.

"That's enough, girls. No sense giving the stuff away. Come on right in, folks. Plenty of time before the big top opens. For one-half of a dollar, four shining bits, you get to see the most beautiful dancing girls in the world, and, in addition, of course, there is also Ramanez, the fireeater; Dumpling Dolly, the tattooed lady; and Tiny Tim, the world's smallest living human being. All on the inside. All waiting to entertain you for a measly one-half of a dollar. One-half of a dollar buys nothing anymore, but here it can buy you one admission to the greatest beauties, wonders, and curiosities that the world can offer. And in addition, at no extra cost, you get to see Grushka, the dancing bear, the only dancing bear in any American tent show, and flown here at great expense from the Balkan forest. You've heard about them, maybe you've seen them on television, now see a dancing bear alive in person."

"To hell with the bear," one of the farmers called out. "I want to see one of them dancing girls bare."

The rest of the crowd began to laugh, and a man behind me said, "That's Jed for you. He knows what he wants. Hey, give me a swig of what you're drinking, Jed."

"Don't touch it, Fred. Jed's moonshine is enough to make a rattlesnake blind."

The man on the platform leaned over and whispered confidentially to Jed that Jed's wish would probably be gratified, and Jed struck his friend in the side and slapped a fifty-cent piece down on the counter. The man with the bottle of Jed's moonshine said that he had seen the show once before, and the girls stripped all the way down to two band-aids and a cork. A few farmers in short sleeves pushed in front of the crowd, and pretty soon the ticket taker was doing a pretty good business. The man behind me, who had a red handkerchief tied around his neck and a white Panama hat in his left hand, was trying to convince his wife to see the show.

"I'm not gong to take the children to see something like that," the wife kept saying. "You ought to be ashamed of yourself."

"What the hell wrong is it to want to see a dancing bear."

"I want to see the dancing bear, Momma," one of their little girls said.

"Now you hush up," the wife said to the girl.

"See, didn't I tell you?" the man with the Panama hat answered. "The girls want to see the dancing bear."

I told Gerry that I thought we should save our money for the main show, but Gerry wanted to see the bear and the fire-eater. She also pointed out that my two friends had joined the fringes of the crowd. They had wandered over to see the dancing girls, but Jackie had stepped on a piece of glass, and now both of them were sitting in the dirt trying to clean the cut. Jackie was crying quite loudly, and the man on the platform became quite annoyed. He told them to go away. "My friend hurt his foot, mistah."

"Why don't you take the girls for some of the rides," said the man with the hat. "I'll meet you by the ponies in about a half an hour."

"So this is what you bring me to the circus for?"

"How often do we ever see a circus? All I want to do is see the sideshow." His wife scowled at him. "Look, you can't believe what Jed said about the girls. Jed ain't never seen it either, and that guy out front just says it to get them to go inside."

"Worked on you, didn't it?" the wife said.

"Hey," the man on the platform said to Jackie's friend, "out behind the big top is a small white tent with a cross on it. You'll find the vet there. He's a good doctor. Let him take a look at it."

"I ain't got no money for a doctor."

"Just get going. He won't charge you nothing. You're blocking the traffic."

"Does the doc inspect the women, too?" Jed yelled, and the crowd laughed again.

"We better go if we're going," Gerry suggested. "Or else it'll be too late."

"O.K." The farmer in front of me placed a bottle of Jed's moonshine into the side pocket of his jeans, and Gerry and I followed him into the tent.

"Come on in, folks. Only one-half of a dollar to see the world's greatest magicians, fire-eaters, and freaks. Plenty of time to see the whole show."

It took me a few minutes to get my eyes accustomed to the change of light, but Gerry spotted the fire-eater, and we walked over to where he was performing. Ramanez was dressed as a Mexican cowboy, complete with black chaps and with a black sombrero hanging around his neck. He took two wire coat hangers out of a tin can, wrapped some cotton around them, dipped them into kerosene, and set them on fire. He threw his head back and quickly placed his mouth around the flame. The crowd applauded politely, but the farmer in front of me said, "I bet he can't eat my wife's cooking." Everyone laughed, except Ramanez, of course. He merely glared straight at the crowd.

"Ramanez can eat anything," he said.

Ramanez swallowed a few more flaming coat hangers, and, at the end of his act, he brought forth some postcards to sell to the crowd. The postcard was a picture of himself swallowing a huge torch of fire. "Senors and senoritas, only one thin valueless dime, and you may purchase this valuable souvenir. We could have charged every person twice the price of admission to see this show, but we don't because we want children to get in, too. That's why we don't charge so much. But if you would like to help us and keep us from raising our price of admission, you can do so by purchasing such things as these postcards. Only ten cents. They make a perfect souvenir. Send them to your friends who couldn't come to the circus and show them what they missed."

One of the farmers bought a couple of cards, and the rest of the crowd wandered off in different directions. "I'm going to send one of these to Barney," Jed said. "Barney'll get a big kick out of it. A real fire-eater, heh. Hah, hah. Barney'll eat his heart out."

"Last chance to get these souvenirs," Ramanez said. "You can't get them anywhere else in the world, but here. Senors and senoritas, listen."

On the other side of the tent, next to a sign advertising the tattooed lady, a magician stepped forward on a raised platform. He wasn't dressed as a magician, though. He simply rolled up the sleeves of his white shirt and announced he was going to show some tricks, and some of the kids gathered around.

"Look closely," he said. "Step closer, folks, so I can impress your sights and senses with fascinating feats of legerdemain and prestidigitation."

"Hell, no use for me to watch this," the man named Jed said. "I don't even understand what he's talking about."

The man in the shirt sleeves took a cigarette out of his mouth and placed it into his fist. When he slowly opened his fingers, the cigarette had disappeared.

"Do you know how he did it?" Gerry asked.

"I think so," I said.

"Tell me."

"No."

"Why not."

"It's a secret."

Gerry looked at me coldly but I didn't say anything. One of the farmers took a drink from Jed's bottle, and Jed said that he could make more cigarettes disappear in a week than the magician could make disappear in a year. Everybody knew that was true too, because Jed smoked a helluva a lot. I offered Gerry a cigarette, and she took it, which surprised me some, because she didn't usually smoke in public. Next, the man showed four kings. He made a wave of his hand and the four kings changed to aces. Next he showed a picture of a woman by placing a flashlight behind the paper; he made it seem that the woman was wiggling her hips. Then he turned the paper slightly, and it looked as if the woman was naked. A couple of the farmers whistled and said how they would like to own something like that.

"Did I hear someone say that they'd like to know how these tricks are done?" the man on the platform said. "Well, here I'm going to show you that anybody can do these tricks. All you got to do is have the equipment. See, this is the handy-dandy vanisher. Just stick a cigarette in it, let go slightly, and the cigarette will disappear out of sight.

"Quit hogging the bottle, Sal. I paid for half of it," the man in the Panama hat said.

"I ain't hogging it."

"Well, give it along."

"Did you see how that was done?" Sal asked.

"Yeah, I saw it. You think I'm blind."

"Well, I want to buy one of those things."

"Now just hold your horses," the magician said. "I'm going to sell the whole kit-and-caboodle for one-tenth the price it would cost you in the city. Now look at these special cards here. All you got to do is turn them around and kings change to aces. And if you buy this paper dancer here, you can have her strip for you anytime you want to. So simple. Just by folding the paper. Now I tell you what I'm going to do. I could sell any of these for a dollar apiece, but you've been such a good audience that I'm going to let you have all these tricks for a dollar. Three tricks, including the instruction. Come on, get them while they last. Fool your friends with them."

"Lend me a dollar, Jed."

"All I ever do is lend you money. Ain't you ever going to repay me?"

"Come on, hand me a buck."

"I tried to call you last night," I said to Gerry.

Gerry untied the ribbon around her hair, shook her hair back and forth, and then retied it. "So," she said.

"So you weren't in."

"I didn't say I would be."

"I ain't going to give you the money," Jed said, "unless you teach me to do the tricks too."

"Give me that goddamn bottle back," Sal said.

"No, you didn't," I answered. I put my hand on Gerry's shoulder, but she walked away from me. "I want to see the dancing bear," she said.

"I don't know where it is."

"Only one dollar buys you the world's greatest feats of the world's greatest magicians."

"So where were you last night?" I asked.

"It's a secret. You won't tell me how the tricks are done." Gerry began walking toward the platform where the dancing girls were assembled. The man who had been out front was setting up the record player again.

"You can buy them for a dollar." I said.

"I don't have a dollar."

"Damn it, I'll buy them for you," I told her, and I went back to the magician's platform.

"Hell, I can't make heads or tails of these directions," old Jed was saying.

"A lousy buck doesn't entitle you to private lessons," the man on the platform said.

"Here's a buck. Let me have one of these." I handed him the money and he gave me a packet of tricks. I brought them to Gerry, but she wouldn't take them..

"Keep them for yourself," she said. "What am I going to do with them?"

"Take them. I bought them for you."

"No."

The girls were dancing now, but they had a difficult time because the record was scratched, and it kept skipping in places. Every once in a while, one of the girls would uncover her breasts, and the farmers would hoot and whistle. "Come on, girls. You got more than that to show us," the man with the Panama hat said.

"Ain't your wife and children waiting for you, Joe?"

"Let them wait. I ain't seen no circus in a long time."

"Let's go," I said to Gerry, but she didn't move. "What's wrong?" I asked.

"Nothing," she said. "I want to see the show."

"Gawd, ain't that girl got a nice pair of boobs? I ain't seen a show like this since I was in Chicago."

"When were you in Chicago?"

"I was there right after the war."

"Which war you talking about? The war between the states?" Everybody liked the joke.

The women danced for about fifteen minutes, and then the man in the white shirt turned off the record player.

"Hey, is that all we get for our money?" the man named Sal said. "Outside you said we'd get to see all they got."

"Well, you still can. Now look. This is a family show. Women and children are in here. So this is just the family part of the show. Now all you have to do, if you want to now, is just go through this entranceway here to the private show. And when I say private show, I mean private show. No women or children allowed. Nobody under eighteen is allowed."

"I ain't under eighteen," Joe said.

"Why don't you get back to your wife and kids?"

"Why in the hell don't you shut up."

"Now quit your quarreling," the man in the white shirt said. "For one small dollar you can feast your eyes on the most tempting delights ever offered to man since the Garden of Eden. See such dancing as you never seen before. Art for art's sake."

"It ain't my eyes I want to get on 'em."

"You didn't say nothing about no extra dollar outside," Jed complained.

"And it didn't cost you no extra dollar for this show, did it? What I'm talking about is the private extra show. You didn't think the girls were going to show off for the women and children, did you? What do you want me to do, get in trouble with the law? I didn't come this far south to corrupt no youth. I'm here to cater to them that already knows better."

"Well, goddamn it, I just wasted my dollar on a bunch of magic tricks." Jed spat on the sawdust.

"It's not my fault. This is your once-in-a-lifetime chance. If you don't want to take advantage of it, it's up to you. Come on, men. You can believe what I'm telling you. This is the hottest show south of the Mason-Dixon Line. And the whole thing starts in ten minutes. Just long enough to let the girls get out of their costumes, if you get what I mean."

On the other side of the tent, someone announced a performance involving a dancing bear, so some of the women and children walked off in that direction. The men didn't move.

"Hey, Joe, loan me a buck, and I won't tell the little woman on you."

"I told you before," Joe said. "Shut the hell up! I wouldn't lend you a buck unless you were buying your coffin."

"There's a good movie at the drive-in," I said to Gerry. "You want to go tomorrow night?"

"No."

"Why not?"

"I have to stay home."

"Hell, for a buck you'd sell your mother down river," Jed said.

"And for another buck you'd be down there waiting for her."

"Come on, gentlemen, set up and see the wickedest little show ever to come south."

A few more dollars changed hands, and Joe finally broke down and lent his friend some money. "What those northern girls got that our girls ain't?"

"Nothing," the man in the shirt sleeves answered. "Except this afternoon you'll just get to see a little more of it."

Gerry was bored with the jokes, so we walked over toward the dancing bear. I felt sorry that she didn't have any shoes on, for I wouldn't have walked barefoot through that sawdust for all the money in the world.

On the platform, a man and a woman led forward a large brown bear. They placed the bear on a bicycle that had two beginner's wheels attached to the back, and the bear rode it around for a while. The bear had a muzzle on, but I guess it could have been pretty dangerous if it wanted to.

"JOE! Are you in there?" Joe's wife was out front, and she was shouting for her husband. "Joe, come out here this instant!"

"Oh, Joe. Oh, Joe. Come out here, Joe," people in the tent started cooing.

The people on the platform were now playing catch with the bear, tossing a bright red beach ball back and forth. "Maybe we could go some other time," I said, but Gerry didn't answer. She just kept looking at the bear. "I wonder if they can train grizzly bears," she said.

The people on the platform had dressed the bear up like one of the dancing girls, and, when the music started, the bear went through the motions of dancing. The crowd hooted and hollered. Even the children laughed and clapped their hands. It was the high spot of the show.

"If she can cook, I'll marry the animal," someone in the crowd said.

"Joe, where are you?" The plaintive call of Joe's wife brought more laughter from the crowd.

"I don't want to see you anymore," Gerry said.

On the platform, the bear was placed on a large medicine ball, and he began balancing on it, rolling it back and forth. "What?" I said, but the air was going out of me.

"Joe, I'm going home."

"Look, be quiet, lady," someone said. "Joe can't hear you. He's inside with the naked women."

"Why not?" I asked. I wanted to reach out and touch her, but I couldn't. The bear was dancing again. Maybe the owners couldn't think of enough variety for the act.

"It's not your fault," Gerry said.

"It's Tom Hendrix, isn't it?"

The man on the platform tied boxing gloves on the bear's paws, and then tied some gloves on himself. They sparred a bit, and the crowd laughed and shouted. The kids didn't get to see that kind of stuff very often, so it was pretty special to them.

"So that's where you were last night."

Gerry didn't answer. I looked at her face and her figure, and when I turned back toward the stage, the bear was gone. After the owners took a final bow, the magician came back to the platform. This time he wheeled in a long, red wooden box and carried a number of steel blades.

"What do you want to do?" I asked.

On the other side of the tent there was a slight commotion because Joe's wife was trying to enter the private dance show, and the man who was the fire-eater before refused to let her enter. "If you don't let me see my husband," she screamed, "I'll call the cops. And my brother is a cop. I'll get this sex carnival closed down, that's what I'll do."

"Now calm down, ma'am. Everything'll be all right. You just describe what he looks like and I'll get him," he said.

"Well he's got more money than I'll ever have," I said.

"You ass," Gerry said.

"All right, gather in close," the magician on the platform

announced. "I'm going to show you one of the most exciting things you've ever seen in your life. My assistant here, and you can all see how beautiful she is, is going to get in this red coffin here, and I'm going to push six steel blades through her body." The magician's assistant stepped forward, with a robe wrapped about her.

"I want to go in with you," Joe's wife said. "I'm not going to wait out here."

"It's against the rules, ma'am." The fire-eater called over one of the refreshment men, and the refreshment men disappeared into the private tent. "It's only a dance back there, but the rules are the rules."

"How long has it been going on?" I asked. "You slept with him, didn't you?"

"Now let me tell you something about my assistant," the magician said. "This red coffin here is so thin that it is impossible for my assistant to fit inside it with many clothes on. She has to take off all her clothes before she can get into the coffin, and so she doesn't have anything at all under her robe. She's going to climb into this box, and then I'm going to pierce her flesh with these hard, cold steel blades. And just to prove that there is no trickery going on, you will be invited to come up onto this platform to look for yourself."

The assistant walked over to the red box, and the magician opened the top. The assistant climbed into the box, and the magician helped her off with her robe, but he held it in such a way that no one could see too much of her as she climbed in. "Yes, ladies and gentlemen, she is in there just as nature made her. Now I'm going to place these steel blades through the coffin and through her." He held up one steel blade and placed it into a prepared slot. He pushed the blade down, until it was possible to see part of the blade protruding from the bottom of the coffin.

"You never slept with me," I said.

"I didn't want to," she said.

"That's obvious."

"I'm going to meet Tom. Thanks for inviting me anyway."

"Yeah. Thanks. I thought you said he was dating one of the

girls in the show?"

Gerry turned and went through the crowd. The shorts she wore were so tight that they didn't leave much to the imagination. "Be careful of the broken glass out front," I said. "I know a boy who cut his foot."

On stage, the man had finished driving the last of the steel blades through the woman's body. "All right, fiends," he called, "it's difficult to believe that my assistant is still in there, but she is. She's in there just as God made her. Now all you have to do is pay one thin dime to come up to the platform and see for yourself that she's still in there. One thin dime. That's all it costs for you to satisfy your curiosity."

Some of my friends from high school began lining up on the platform, and since I didn't have to buy any tickets for the main show, I decided to throw away a dime and go up and take a look. I gave the guy my dime and walked by the coffin, but the people behind me were impatient, so I couldn't take my time. It was difficult to see much of her, for she was on her side, and somehow she had managed to wind her body around the blades. I guess she had been pretty once. Gerry was much prettier, but then Gerry was younger.

When I left the tent, I looked to see if Gerry was still outside, but she wasn't. She had probably entered the main tent. I didn't know what I would do if I saw them.

"Hey mistah, what's you got in your hand?"

"Huh?"

"What's you got?"

It was Boston Blackie again and his friend Jackie. "Oh, it's you two again. How's your friend's foot?"

"It's okay. The veterinarian put some horse liniment on it."

"That's good."

"Where's your girl?"

"She's not my girl. We were just kidding you."

"Oh."

The men began filing out of the side tent. Sal was so drunk

that he had to be held up by his friends. Joe's wife had returned to her husband's truck and stood waiting with the children. Joe walked slowly over to join them. "I owe you a buck, ol' buddy," Sal cried. "Believe me, I won't forget. Sal don't forget his friends. Ain't that right, Jed? Ain't that right?"

"You still ain't tol' me what you got," my friend said.

"Just some magic tricks." I started to walk through the makeshift parking lot, with cars and trucks parked haphazardly in the field. The two kids followed me.

"Did you buy it, mistah?"

"Yeah, I bought it," I said.

"I thought you said you ain't got no money."

"I don't."

"Then how did you buy that?"

"You want it?" I asked. "Here, take it." I handed him the packet of tricks.

"How about fifty cents so we can go see the snake," Boston Blackie demanded, "Jackie and me'd rather see the snake."

"That's life," I said.

Jackie ripped open the package and took out some of the cards and the secret vanisher. "Hey, man," Boston Blackie said. "What good is this stuff without learning us how to do it." The kid named Jackie began to cry.

"What's he crying for," I said. We had walked so far that the tents seemed a long way off. We were on the very edge of the parking lot.

"It's his foot. He's been crying all afternoon. Don't pay no attention to him. He's a crybaby."

"You better go back to the circus," I suggested, "before you get lost. Maybe you can sell the tricks to somebody so you can see the snake."

"Why don't you learn us how to do them."

"The instructions are included," I said. I kept walking away.

"Me and Jackie can't read."

"Tough. For free you don't get lessons." I quickened my pace and left them behind, with the kid called Jackie crying his head off.

"Besides you never even told me your real name."

"You know, you're a real big spender," Boston Blackie said.

"Take your friend to a good doctor before his foot gets infected," I shouted back. I turned around to face them and saw the little tents with their bright flags blowing back and forth in the wind. Most of the kids were arriving from school, so the lot was beginning to fill up. "Maybe I'll see you next year."

"Yeah, sure. See ya next year."

"Yeah, next year. Maybe." How anybody could have walked through that field in bare feet was more than I could understand.

# REAL CRIMES

The first time I returned home from college was a sad time in 1960. The period was sad because I had to leave behind a girlfriend in Pennsylvania. Sad because it was a harsh winter. Sad because Thomas Wolfe had been right about not going home again. I had gone to college in Philadelphia, and had not gone home for more than a year. I didn't have enough money to go home. My parents would have been happy to come up with a bus ticket, but they didn't have much money either. It was a year in which all the money in the world had vanished. You could stand all day looking up at the sky and know that nothing in the air was promising very much. Thus, I had let my life meander longer than I should have. I had spent my first Christmas away from home at my girlfriend's house. It was as if I had been a foreign student, and I guess in many ways I was. A couple of my friends felt the same way. Some didn't. Quite a few times that first year I told myself that I had no business to go away to college. It was expensive, and what did Pennsylvania mean to me? What did I mean to Pennsylvania? Philadelphia, the City of Brotherly Love. What a crock!

My father, in those days, owned a Sunoco filling station in Clarkston, Georgia, and if I knew one thing about my life, I knew this: I didn't want to end up like my old man—pumping gas, wiping windows, changing tires, cleaning vomit off the toilets, overseeing the prophylactic machines, and trying to figure out what to do with the Green Stamp people when they came by with their wild stories about how Green Stamps were going to attract customers like crazy. Everybody wants something for free, and in the time I'm talking about, my father had to practically torture people to get them to buy Sunoco. Half the stations in Clarkston were giving away everything but the kitchen sink, and one was offering a free trip to Bermuda, to get cars to drive in and fill-'er-up. It was like that then, though nobody under twenty is ever going to believe it.

Specifically, I'm talking about a time in December when I came home from good old Penn. Those first days at home were pretty much the same for everyone–uneasy greetings, awkward pauses, prolonged pauses, feverish attempts to get caught up on the whereabouts of anybody you remotely knew. I had been home for about a week when one of my former teachers called suggesting that we get together for a drink. God knows I needed to get out of the house. The television was going thirty hours a day, and my father was nagging at me to get down to the gas station and help out with the crowds. Crowds? Five people were to him a crowd.

As for my former ex-teacher, he was a short, fat man named Giscombe Palmer. It really wasn't much of a usable name in a town like Clarkston. That summer after high school, when time lay like a sack of concrete on my head, I had taken up golf with a vengeance. My teacher and I had played many a round together and, because of my new status in the world, I could call him Lee, short for Leland, his middle name. His mother had a knack of laying on the names. My own name is Clifford Conover, in case anybody asks.

The temperature had dropped to the high thirties, and the local orange growers were putting the smudge pots out into the groves, when Lee drove up in his beat-up Buick. I crossed the front yard to greet him. I was taken aback to notice just how much weight Old Lee had lost. I call him "Old Lee" because he was in his mid-forties. I had left him fat and returned to find him thin, just as I had left my parents when they seemed young, and returned to find them gray. But, as I said, Old Lee was in his mid-forties and he was already losing his hair. He was dressed in a blue sweater and green slacks. My mother invited him inside for a drink. It was quite an occasion to have one's old English teacher visit the house. If you're anything like me, you have a difficult time imagining what a teacher looks like outside of the classroom. You wonder if some of them are human at all and if they have any existence twenty yards beyond the blackboard.

Old Lee had a human existence all right. Around the high school, he had a reputation for flirting with the girls, but if anything went on beyond flirting, I never knew. Lee had taught at Clarkston High for almost a decade, and the kids liked him because he was always joking. He knew I liked to write, and I guess that's why we got along. If Lee had his choice, he would have quit teaching in a minute and would have gone off to play golf somewhere and write the Great American Novel, but he had eight kids at home. Eight kids kept him tied down. Eight kids could tie down an elephant. I also knew Old Lee didn't get along with his wife. Still, he had eight kids, which means to my mind that he was not ignoring her every night. Oh, but he could stand up in a room filled with people and tell them his adventures of raising a world filled with Catholics on a schoolteacher's salary. He would have everyone in stitches. He could make my mother laugh until tears rolled out of her eyes and down her cheeks. But when you get Old Lee off by himself in a bar, you knew it was no joke at all. He owned an ulcer you could sail to Europe on. It was Poverty City he had moved in on and had taken up residence in.

That winter night in my parent's living room, Old Lee clutched his glass of milk and kept my parents laughing. He was alive that night, and I didn't find out why until we made our getaway, taking off for adventures in his beat-up Buick. To be frank about it, Old Lee's car was a mess. The back seat was strewn with coloring books, crayons, newspapers, books, and candy wrappers. He could have hidden two or three kids back there. Ask Old Lee how many kids he had, and he would always say the same thing: eight that I know of, six or seven others scattered—two somewhere in the back seat. In the trunk were his golf clubs. He carried his clubs with him; he never knew, he said, when he might want to get out and take a practice swing or try a new grip. How he saved up the money to buy a set of golf clubs, I'll never know. He was always selling something—encyclopedias, radios, fountain pens. There were days at school when he was a regular walking inventory. But he had charm. He could have sold ice to the Eskimos if he had wanted to.

As we turned on to U.S.1, a light rain fell. "Want to do me a favor?" he said at last.

"What kind of favor?"

"Come with me to Paula's. You can be my excuse."

I had heard about Paula the summer before, so he didn't have to say anything more. That's the way it is with friends. They say one or two words, and your lifetimes fill in the rest.

"All right," I said. If his wife called the house, my parents would say that Old Lee and I were out together. To be frank about it, I was annoyed, but on the other hand, I figured what the hell. I didn't have anything else to do. It wasn't as if I wanted to sit home all night, staring at Pantomime Quiz.

"Don't look like that," Old Lee said. "You'll like Paula. I've certainly told her enough about you."

The rain was falling a bit heavier now, but his windshield wipers were on the blink. Nothing Old Lee owned ever worked right. How he got eight kids, I never knew. "I didn't say I wouldn't like her, did I?"

Lee didn't answer the question. "She's got a daughter who is anxious to meet you."

Lee always knew somebody who was anxious to meet me. "How old?" I asked.

"Sixteen."

I didn't say anything to that. I merely fiddled with the black knobs on the car radio. The radio didn't work either. Lee waited for an answer, and so I said, "Why don't I rob the cradle while I'm at it." The rain on the windshield was making it difficult to see where we were going.

"Her name is Cheryl, and she's got a body that will drive you crazy. She looks a lot older than you think."

Old Lee stopped for a light and stepped out of the car to run the windshield wipers back and forth by hand. It helped a bit. I sat very still and thought about Camus. Lee and I had talked about Camus a lot. One more reason why we got along. Camus' death was a real crime. A streak of existentialism through the two of us ran a mile wide and a mile deep. That's what going off to Pennsylvania had done to me; I don't know what going to college had done for him. In my senior year at Clarkston, Old Lee had shown me some essays he had written, essays in which he embraced atheism and renounced God. What do I think? I think that renouncing God is easy. Getting out of an evening with a sixteen-year-old girl you have never met, now that's what takes some doing.

"She looks like dynamite," he said. "I wish I were your age." The Buick pulled into a gravel driveway. A shaggy black-haired dog with brown spots on its face barked out to greet us. A door pushed open. "Get out of here, you crazy mutt," Lee shouted. He got out of the Buick and waved the dog back. The mutt retreated to its place under the porch. If you have handled teenagers in classrooms all your life, intimidating wild dogs must come easily.

Under the yellow lights of the porch stood a slender girl in a pink blouse and black slacks that were skintight. She couldn't get any more into them without splitting them open. Lee and I walked up. Lee went first. I followed. "Cheryl, this is the guy I was telling you about." It wasn't eloquent, but it got the job done. At least she knew who I was. Cheryl didn't look up.

"The swimming champ?" she asked, her jaw going a mile a minute with the gum in it. She stood five feet five or six, with her black hair tied into a ponytail. Her figure said that she was grown-up beyond her years. Who was Lee kidding? I thought. Cheryl is no sixteen. Paula had been lying about her daughter's age to make herself look younger in my friend's eyes.

Lee gave Cheryl a tender tap on the back of her head. "No. Not the swimmer, Dummy. That was a high-school kid. Cliff's home from college."

I thought that would make an impression on her, but it didn't. With her bare feet, Cheryl formed circles of dust on the porch. Her nails on both feet and both hands were polished bright red. Her lipstick was on thick and juicy. "I thought you were the swimmer," she said to nobody in particular.

Lee pushed opened the door. "Paula inside?" He didn't stay for a reply. The door shut behind him. I wasn't comfortable standing on the porch. In fact, I had been looking forward to meeting the great passion of Lee's life. Everybody is entitled to one great passion, he had said. Paula was his. I hadn't met my great passion yet, but then I was younger than Old Lee. I had my whole life ahead of me.

"Aren't you cold? I mean, standing out here without a sweater?" I asked Cheryl.

"No," she said. "I like it when it's cold." She removed her chewing gum and tossed it into the yard. I could hear the dog breathing under the porch. "Don't you hate the summers down here when everything's so hot and sticky that you have to change your clothes three or four times a day?" She finally looked up. The yellow light bulb swinging overhead was not very flattering to either of us. It gave the appearance we had come down with jaundice. I understood the need of yellow light bulbs in the summer when the air was a molasses river of insects. But in winter? Even if my blood had thickened from being in the north, I was still shivering. It was cold and damp, but I couldn't think of anything more to say about her clothing. "Can we go inside?" I asked.

"What for?"

"I'm not as used to the cold the way you are."

"I bet," she said. She made me feel as if I were being accused of something. "I thought you were a swimmer," she said.

"That's somebody else," I answered, backing toward to the door.

"I bet." She bent down and glanced through the living room window. She had been waiting for my friend and her mother to get settled. "Coffee?"

I nodded. She opened the door and we went inside.

"Coffee, tea, or me?" She smiled. Her teeth were straight and white. Inside, within her own space, she seemed more relaxed, more energetic, though the living room was certainly nothing to brag about. Paula's house resembled the back seat of Old Lee's Buick. My mother could have had a field day cleaning it, ordering vacuum cleaners through it like tanks chasing the Desert Fox. There were papers and detective magazines on the floor. Against the cream-colored wall that needed a good scrubbing stood a solitary sofa, faded and forlorn. There was an over-stuffed chair covered with doilies. A crumpled plaid blanket lay upon it. In front of the sofa there was a small glass table supported by white wrought-iron legs. The table belonged outside, but it had been dragged inside for the winter. The door to Paula's bedroom was closed.

I took the sofa and picked up a copy of *True Detective*. A woman in bra and panties was tied to a motel room bed. A man with a knife stood over her. Good stuff, I thought. Directly across from me stood a small black-and-white television set balanced precariously upon a portable metal stand. Cheryl brought in the coffee and placed the mugs on the glass table. The top three buttons of her pink blouse were undone. When she bent over, I helped myself to a look at her own white bra. Her breasts were not large, but they would have warmed me nicely. "Don't mind the stupid magazine," she said, moving some schoolbooks away. "My mother is trying to sell some stories."

The coffee was fragrant and strong. "Any luck?"

"Naah. It's a tough market."

"I thought they were supposed to be true crimes," I said, trying not to look down her blouse.

"Are you kidding?" She was fidgeting with the cushions, lifting one up to see if she had lost anything. "There are more murders in this neighborhood than you can count. In back of the trailer court down the block, a woman was found tossed in the river, tied down with concrete blocks, her hands cut off." Her blue eyes were round with the telling. I moved closer to her.

"I believe you," I said, putting down the coffee.

"I bet." She replaced the cushion. I moved my face close to hers. She didn't move away. I moved my mouth close to her mouth. She didn't move away. I kissed her for a long time. I tried to place my tongue inside her mouth, but she pulled back. "You want to hear the rules?" she asked.

"What rules?"

"My rules."

"Sure. Go ahead." No one had laid down rules before. I looked at the clock resting on the kitchen table. Ten-thirty. Lee wouldn't be able to stay all night because he had a wife to get back to. Every once in a while, Cheryl and I could hear sounds of lovemaking from behind the closed door. I don't know why I was being punished. I had no wife to get back to.

"No frenching," she said. "No petting below the waist. No taking off my clothes. No going into the bedroom. O.K.?"

After all that, it certainly didn't make sense to go into the bedroom. "What should I do," I asked, "call in a professional arbitrator?"

"I'm just telling you the rules, that's all." She stretched out full-length upon the couch. I stretched out full-length next to her, and we kissed. I could fondle her brassiere all I wanted to, but she wouldn't let me touch her below the waist. Both of us were talking in near whispers, as if we were co-conspirators in some crime, although I wasn't quite certain what the crime should be. In America in those days you always felt guilty kissing some girl you weren't going to marry. My head was spinning. There was a great ache between my legs.

We kissed. Her lipstick was moist and sweet. For a few minutes I held her head between my hands and then her neck. Her skin was smooth, and I could not take my mouth away. Her body pressed against mine. My hands roamed under her blouse. I could not take my hands away. She was not teasing me, I thought. She was just being what she was. As soon as I undid her brassier, she sat up, refastened it, and then returned to kissing me as if nothing at all had happened, and maybe it hadn't. Outside, the spotted dog was barking at someone next door.

Cheryl wasn't going to change her mind. To keep from losing mine, I broke free and stood up. "Let's go in there," I whispered, pointing toward her bedroom.

"Wanna bet?" she asked. She didn't sit up. I

I walked away and paced the room. I looked out the window. It had stopped raining, and a moon was beginning to appear.

"I can put more coffee on," she volunteered.

"Wanna bet?" I said. "I don't need any more stimulation."

She laughed. It wasn't a mean laugh. It was just a laugh. I liked her well enough. "I told you the rules before we started," she said. I couldn't argue with that, though many rules in life are meant to be broken.

"A crime against nature," I said. "How old are you?"

"Fifteen."

"Fifteen!" I repeated. "You don't look fifteen."

"I know," she said matter-of-factly. "You a big man of the world?"

"I'm not even a swimmer."

"You're funny," she said.

"I know." I picked up her schoolbooks and riffled the pages. "These your books?"

"Not my mother's." She sat up and held out her hand. I gave her her book. "If you weren't here," she said, "I'd be studying."

I nodded. It didn't strike me as a kind thing to say. The clock on the kitchen table said 11:15. I wondered how much longer Old Lee was going to indulge his sex life. He was getting more out of the evening than I was.

"We gotta read about the Jews, and I hate them," Cheryl said.

"The Jews?"

"Yeah. You know." She opened the book and spread the pictures across the coffee table. I know. What was I going to say? That I didn't? "How Hitler put millions of them to death in concentration camps." She looked up from a picture of naked skeletons staring out from behind barbed wire. "You Jewish?" she asked.

"Who? Me?"

"Yeah, you."

"No," I lied. Half-lied because my grandfather on my father's side had been Jewish.

"I bet."

"If you're a Jew and you deny it, it's a crime against God," I said.

"Big deal."

"What? A crime against God?"

"God doesn't exist. So how can anyone commit crimes against him?"

"I don't know. I'm not a lawyer," I said. She sounded as if she had been talking to Old Lee.

"Anyway, I could tell you weren't Jewish."

"I didn't think we had gone that far," I said bitterly, wondering if she'd even caught my sarcasm. I went into the kitchen to warm up the coffee. I had decided to give Old Lee fifteen more minutes, and that would be it.

"Conover is not a Jewish name," she said.

"I agree with you there."

She looked through her book. I studied the coffee. There was talking of sorts from Paula's bedroom. "Anyway I'm glad you're not a Jewy Dewy," she said. "They're all so dumb."

"I always heard they were smart."

Cheryl squirmed. "There were millions of them, and they just stood by and let the Germans kill them."

"You mean the Nazis. There were German Jews."

"Whatever. They should have put up more of a fight."

"It's not so easy to fight off a highly trained, mechanized army."

My words were falling on deaf ears. Cheryl was too busy unwrapping a new stick of gum to listen to me. She allowed the tin foil to fall to the floor. "I can't even stand to look at the stupid pictures," she said at last. "They make me sick to my stomach." She closed the book with a thud.

Making myself right at home, I rinsed out the coffee mugs and poured myself a cup. It was too late for me to drink coffee, but I had to do something. I wished I had driven my parents' car, for I was beginning to feel like a prisoner myself. "You don't have to read that trashy book," I advised. "You could get yourself a more respectable history."

"In this town? Christ, we're lucky to get *True Detective.*"

I returned with my hot mug of coffee and placed it on the glass-topped table. "Besides, I've been lying to you," I told her. "I really am Jewish. My father converted for the sake of my mother."

"I bet," she said.

I shrugged. I didn't care if she believed me or not. Cheryl, who had been stretched out on the couch with the book of atrocities held high in the air, now sat up and looked into my face. She wanted to see if I was kidding her or not.

"True," I said.

She pulled out a long string of gum and allowed it to snap back. "Well, if it's true, you're in a lot of trouble."

"That right?"

"You've committed a crime against God," she said, smiling. "Besides, I don't care. It's just that I don't want to have to read about the dumb Jews, that's all. I mean, if they didn't let it happen, then I wouldn't have to read about it, that's all." She stood up and crossed to her mother's closed bedroom door, and she knocked.

"Come in," her mother called. Cheryl went in. I could hear them talking about coffee. Cheryl came out and, leaving the door wide open, went to the kitchen for the coffee I had made. Old Lee called my name, so I went in. The two of them were still in bed, with a single sheet pulled over them. I took it all in great stride.

"I want you to meet Paula," he said. Paula was a dark-haired woman with the whitest skin I had ever seen. It was as if she had never been outside. The way she had the sheet pressed around her, I could make out the form of her body. She was tall and slender with large breasts. I understood why Old Lee had been anxious to visit. I also noticed the mother and daughter resemblance.

Paula held out her hand and I took it. "I hope you've been enjoying your visit," Paula said.

I felt like saying, not as much as Old Lee, but for the sake of manners, I didn't.

Lee was fiddling with a pack of Camels. I turned to him and said, "You've got to be careful about smoking in bed." For some reason, that struck everybody's funny bone. When Cheryl entered with two mugs of my coffee, we were laughing quite loudly.

"Clifford was helping me out by telling me about the dumb Jews," Cheryl told her mother.

"That's nice, honey," Paula said. I thought Old Lee would say something in response, but all he said was, "Are you about ready to go home?" I told him I was.

"All right then. Get out of here so we can get dressed."

Cheryl and I went into the living room, and I pulled her toward me and gave her one long kiss, placing my tongue deep inside her mouth. She didn't resist me.

When Old Lee came out, I turned to him and asked, "Hey, Lee, how many children do you have anyway?"

He sat on the sofa and tied his shoes. He gave the response I had expected. "Eight that I know for sure, and six or seven others scattered, two in the backseat." He laughed, and Paula gave him a playful punch in the shoulder. I wondered if he thought it a crime to bring so many children into such an overpopulated world, but it was too late to get involved in that kind of a discussion. Besides, there was nothing he could do about it. On the way home we let the matter ride.

# WATCHING THE ORANGE MOON TILT LIKE CRAZY

I heard the noon whistle and dragged myself into the house. I washed and sat down to lunch. There were only a few of us, and, although it was cooler by the lunch table than it was outside in the layers of dust that surrounded my tractor, we were sweating hard.

"Young Tom," my partner called to me, "you ever going to amount to anything?"

"I'm going to be just like you," I told him.

"That'll be the day!" My partner chuckled, slapping his hands together as if I had said something worth remembering. His name was Sam Little, and he was in his early fifties, not fat, but built solid with leathery skin. "You're a good ole boy, that's what you are."

I nodded and took the biscuits. A good ole boy, that's what I was all right. There were only five of us working the plants, but I was the youngest–seventeen going on eighteen–so I was the butt of the jokes. I was saving my money for a car. I was going to get out. Getting out was what I concentrated upon that summer. My plan was to drive cross-country, take my time, see the sights, sell the car in California, and join the navy. Sam had been in the navy himself, but he didn't talk about it much. Mostly we talked about hunting or fishing or tobacco or getting drunk. Mostly we didn't say much, but one night he told me that he had gone over to Springfield to see a doctor and that the doctor had found something. Sam didn't tell me what it was. He didn't know himself. I told him that he wasn't suffering from anything that a good bath wouldn't cure.

Saturday was a half-day in August, and so, after lunch, Sam decided to drive over to see his doctor, to get the results from the tests. I went along for the ride. I was looking for a new job as well as for a new car.

I wasn't comfortable in the truck because Sam was not a good driver. It seemed as if every other day he would drive his truck off the road, turn it over, climb it up a telephone pole, or knock over mailboxes. I doubt if he had a bona fide license, but he didn't care. Jail didn't mean a thing to him. He'd just as soon sleep in a jail as anywhere else. One piss-soaked mattress wasn't too different from another.

It would be easy to say that Sam's problems as a driver stemmed from the fact that he drank too much. His favorite story concerned the time when he was walking home from a bar, and he spotted a power mower sitting in front of Ames Hardware Store. He climbed on board, turned on the ignition, and drove the machine through town, leaving it where it had stalled out—right in the middle of the railroad tracks. When the train bound for New York collided with it, it caused a hell of a racket, waking up the town. The more times Sam told that story, the louder the noise became. In his head, it was a good joke. Or maybe it was a bad joke that had to be turned to good. I didn't see the humor of it myself. Perhaps if I had spent thirty or forty years of my life building and rebuilding tobacco bulks, I might have done something almost as crazy. There is no sure way of measuring another person's craziness. Sam argued that the town needed a good waking up.

But there was another reason Sam Little was a bad driver. For a couple of years he had given up driving altogether in a region where people can't do anything without a car. The machinery had betrayed him badly, and he had lost his faith. One night Sam and I sat out behind the barn, and between drinks he told me about his ex-wife and his two-year-old daughter. She was no longer two, but she had died at that age. He had been driving around the county, bootlegging liquor, and he had his two-year-old daughter sleeping in the back seat. He kept looking back at her, and she was sweating pretty bad. And then when he came back to the car after making a drop, she was dead. He said her name was Lucy. Lucy had been sleeping in the back seat, and there was a small hole in the floorboard. Carbon monoxide had leaked through. As Sam said, as we watched the orange moon tilt crazy because the moon never rose straight up from the horizon like a flower, it doesn't take much carbon monoxide to kill a two-year-old child. Hardly takes much to kill an adult. His wife left him a little while after that. I guess they both went crazy, but I didn't press him for details. In his mind, Lucy was always two years old. Even then, with my brain buzzing, it struck me as strange that people don't grow older after death. A decade or so passed, and Sam returned to the machinery and to religion. And to jokes so filthy it could make a mule cringe.

Sam asked me if I ever thought about Hell. I said, "No." The only thing I knew about Hell was that it was both hot and cold at the same time. People froze. People sweated. I didn't have many details to go on.

"Have you heard about Swedenborg?" he asked me.

"Where's he work?"

"He don't work." He took off the floppy straw hat he wore in the fields. "Don't they teach you nothing in school?"

"No," I told him. "They don't teach me nothing in school." That was the truth.

"I met this girl in Springfield," he said, trying to make the news sound as off-hand as possible. "She introduced me to him."

"Bring him around sometime."

"He's dead."

"I ain't particular."

"He writes all about Hell," Sam said. He didn't take his eyes off the road. He didn't know what to make of my answers, but I was in no particular mood to talk about Hell with him. "I'm not that interested in Hell, " I told him.

"You would be if you listened to Lucy," he said.

"Who's Lucy?"

"The girl over at Springfield." He tried to make it sound as off-hand as possible . Good for him, I thought. Maybe he was having a good time somewhere. All of us deserved a good time sometime.

He decided not to pursue the subject of Hell with me. It was too hot to think, I told him. I got off at the library because I wanted to read the help-wanted ads, but I didn't tell Sam. Sam promised to pick me up on his way back.

I went inside and found a table. Near me was a forty-year-old man in blue jeans and white T-shirt. Like me he had come to the library to take advantage of the newspapers, but he had brought his wife and children with him. Right away I knew that wasn't a good idea. It's hard enough to be out of work when you're alone. When you got people depending upon you, it makes you feel even worse. To be honest, I couldn't be certain that the woman was the man's wife or whether she was just his girlfriend, except she was no girl. She was in her late thirties and had long brown hair that reached to her waist. She was dressed in tight blue shorts and a short- sleeved T-shirt. Her arms and face were freckled. The two boys seemed to be her children. She scrunched up on the chair next to her man. The two boys, maybe five and seven years of age, ran back and forth. They brought books from the shelves.

"Put them books back where you got them," the woman said.

"Ah, Mom ..."

"Sit down and stop running around," the man told them. He was trying to concentrate on the pile of newspapers in front of him. Since he had the newspapers, I went back to the stacks and found a book by Swedenborg. I had to ask the librarian, but between the two of us, we managed to locate one. I brought it back to the table. It would be a good surprise for Sam. The boys were still running around.

"Sit down," the man told them.

"This is a library," the woman said, "not a zoo."

"I'm not in a zoo," the seven-year-old said.

A third boy joined them. "Mark, come here and sit down," the woman told him.

I waited for some newspapers and passed the time by looking over the book.

> What eternal fire is, and what the gnashing of teeth is, which are mentioned in the Word in reference to those whoare in hell, scarcely anyone as yet has known, because the contents of the Word have been thought about only in a material way, and nothing has been known about its spiritual sense. So fire has been understood by some to mean material fire, by others to mean torment in general, by others, remorse of conscience, and others have held that it is mentioned merely to excite terror in the wicked.

Some of it I understood. Some of it I didn't. I was smarter than Sam, so what he made of it, I had no idea. Of course he had some woman to help him. I didn't know what Swedenborg was talking about, but I knew what it was like to be out of work.

"Write them a resumé," the woman told the man. I was more interested in them than the book.

"Send them a resumé, you turd!" he mimicked, taking the pencil from her hand.

"Isn't that what you're supposed to do?" the woman asked. "You gotta send them a resumé."

"There's a children's library upstairs," the boy called Mark said.

"I don't care if Santa Claus is upstairs," the man told them. "You're going to sit here and be quiet."

"Is Santa Claus upstairs?" the other boy asked.

"Of course, I'll send them a resumé," the man told the woman. "Where in the Hell am I going to get a resumé?"

"Make it up." The woman grabbed the picture books from her children's hands and neatly stacked them up in front of her. "That's what everybody else does."

"You turd!" the man said.

The woman didn't answer him.

"I just want to go upstairs," the boy whined.

She turned to the oldest boy. "All you do is whine. Do you do that with your father?"

The oldest boy slid down in his chair, trying to make himself as small as possible.

The woman looked at the man. "They don't do that with their father. They save up their whining for us."

"Larry hit me."

"We could just look at the books upstairs," Mark suggested.

The man folded his newspaper and picked up another. He was getting impatient to find a job. He pointed his finger at the boy called Larry. "The last time we came here, you two ran all over the place."

The air-conditioning was on, but it must have been on its lowest setting, for I was getting very uncomfortable.

"Was I here?" asked Mark.

The man shook his head. His ears were bright red. "Unfortunately no," he said. "But those two ruined it for you."

The woman tossed her head and grabbed her hair. "Those two are always ruining things for everyone." She pulled some pins from her mouth and pushed them into her hair. I wondered if she were freckled all over.

"Is this place air-conditioned?" the man asked.

The woman nodded.

"I don't feel it," the man said. He had a paunch, and his arms were tattooed. A blue eagle on his left arm. A snake on his right. It didn't look very pretty to me. One night in Boston, Sam had gotten drunk and wanted to get tattooed, but I had talked him out of it.

Larry reached for a stack of books. "Just a few minutes, Ma," he pleaded, but the woman slapped his hand away.

"Don't you start whining," she warned him, "or I'll give you something to whine about."

"I want to go upstairs," the boy begged.

"You can't."

"Please!"

"You're such a crybaby, you know that."

"I'm going to go to California," the man said.

The woman thought about it. "What will I do in California?" she asked. There was a cold edge to her voice.

"I'll send for you."

"Where's California?" the five-year-old asked.

"Yeah, yeah, right." The woman's voice dripped with sarcasm.

"You turd!"

"I wasn't even here the last time," the boy called Mark said.

The man pointed his finger at the woman's sons. "Tell it to those two. Not me." He tore a small sheet of paper from a pad and copied an address from the newspaper.

"Let the kids go upstairs," I shouted at them. I couldn't believe I said it. What was wrong with me? I didn't want to make trouble.

The man put down his newspaper. "What did you say?" The kids turned and stared. The youngest boy put three fingers into his mouth. I thought he was too old to do that.

I had to go through with it. "I said why don't you let the kids go upstairs and read the books?"

"It's none of your business," the woman told me.

"I just want to go upstairs," Mark said,

"Shut up!" the woman told him.

The man pushed his chair back and stood up. "I'll handle this," he told them.

"We don't want no fight, Doug."

Doug sauntered over to my table, leaned over, and placed his stubby hand on my book. I got a good look at his tanned and unshaved face. "Would you like to step outside?" he asked. There was liquor on his breath.

"It's all right with me," I said. I shrugged. It didn't make no difference to me.

"Daddy," the seven-year-old whined. The five-year-old sat there with three fingers in his mouth. His brown eyes were large as saucers.

The man called Doug looked hard at the boys. "You all set right there. I'll be right back." He took his hand off my book.

The woman followed us out. She kept calling the man's name over and over, but the man didn't answer. He turned around and pushed her away. I went through the turnstile and went outside. After a little while he came out. We didn't say nothing. I walked around the back of the building and he followed me. "Dumb turd!" he said. If he said it once, he must have said it a thousand times. It's weird how the human mind gets stuck on one note. We stopped in the parking lot.

"What's all this about?" I asked him.

"You tell me."

"Why don't you let the kids go upstairs and read the books?"

"Because they're my kids, that's why," he said, taking off his shirt and draping it in the hood of a car. "What's it to you? Don't you know enough not to butt into somebody else's business?"

I took off my shirt and draped it over the hood of another car. The sun was bearing down on us, and we were both sweating. "You're good at bullying little kids," I told him.

I didn't put up my fists, but he took a swing at me. I stepped back, turning my body, allowing the blow to fall upon my shoulder. It was a good solid punch, but I was in no mood to appreciate the beauty of it. Both of us had a lot of anger. I slapped him back, cuffing his ear, and he went for my ribs. I kicked my right foot forward and tripped him. Maybe it wasn't fair, but that was his problem. His head banged hard on the asphalt. The kids came running out, calling for their father. I jumped on their old man, and now the two of us were rolling around between the cars. Both of our bodies were so covered with sweat that we had a difficult time holding a grip. The back of his head was bleeding, and my shoulder was sore.

"Leave him alone," the kids cried, and then the oldest jumped on my back, and the other two followed.

"Get away, you fucking kids!" Doug shouted. I reached back to slap one off my back. Doug flailed, and his open hand struck Mark in the face. Mark hit the pavement with a thud.

"Oh hell!" I said. The boy's mouth was bleeding. Doug pushed me off and picked up his son. "You all right?" he asked. Mark was crying, and so were the other boys.

To calm them down I said, "We were just fooling along." Of course, they didn't believe me. No one in his right mind could. My elbows were badly skinned, but otherwise I had suffered no damage. My pants were dripping wet.

"Get in the goddamn truck," Doug ordered the kids. "Where's your momma? Did that bitch send you out here?"

The woman had come out of the library. She stood on the edge of the parking lot staring at us. I took my shirt from the car. "I'll give you my phone number," I told him, "if you want to continue this some other time."

"Fuck you!" he said. He took his shirt and carried his son to the truck. The woman and the two younger boys joined him. They climbed into the truck, and I watched them drive off. I didn't feel sorry for them. Fuck 'em! They're all dumb jerks. I put my shirt back on, went back inside the library, found the men's room, and gave myself a good washing. There were no paper towels to be found, so I wiped myself off with my shirt. That's the way the world is. If you need something like paper towels, they're never around. I went back to the reading tables and found the stack of newspapers my friend had been studying.

I needed to get myself a truck like my friend, but felt foolish and alone because I didn't have seven thousand dollars for a Ranger pickup.

Then I saw it: "A Travel Job - No Exerience Needed"

Yeah. That was the key. No experience. "Will hire 10 sharp, outgoing guys and gals to tour Miami, LA, Vegas, Denver, and New York as representatives for leading fashion, music, and sports publication." I'm not outgoing enough. That's my problem. And there is dirt under my fingernails. I was beginning to get upset over the dirt under my fingernails.

Some of the newsprint was coming off on my hands and lower arms. Everything was turning black and damp. I hate that. You turn to the help-wanted ads for help, and you end up stained for life. Maybe that was what the Old Testament meant by the mark of Cain. I continued reading. Cain looking for a new brother. Immediate opening.

I studied the large round clock over the magazine racks. Sam had told me that he would pick me up at three o'clock. The clock said five. It wasn't like Sam to be on time, but it wasn't like him to be two hours late. Sam hadn't told me the name of his doctor. He hadn't told me the name of the hospital where he had been going for tests. He was willing to talk religion, but he was pretty closed mouth about the rest of his life. When he got drunk, he would reach back and drag out Lucy sleeping in the back seat forever. About five-thirty, I called Consolidated. Ruby answered.

"Have you seen Sam?" I asked her.

"Was I supposed to?" she asked. Ruby was the wife of the man who ran the tobacco farm for Consolidated. She was a fat jolly lady who cooked up a storm.

"I'm calling from Springfield," I told her. I didn't tell her where I was because I didn't want her to know what I was up to. She and her husband wanted me to work for them forever. "Sam was supposed to pick me up two hours ago. I thought maybe he might have forgotten all about me and gone on home."

"Hold on," she said. She dropped the receiver so that it clucked against the wooden stand. I searched my pants for coins. When Ruby returned, she said, "No. Nobody around here has seen him. Everybody says he went off with you."

"I know that," I said. Ruby was always telling me the obvious. Everything seemed more obvious to me than ever. "I've been waiting for him over two hours."

She thought about that. "You want me to send someone after you?"

"No," I said. "It's too much trouble."

"It will get Bobby out of my hair for a while."

"No. I'll hitch back. If that sonuvabitch Sam drives in, tell him he forgot somebody, and he's going to get his ass kicked from here to kingdom come." I hung up and decided to go outside to wait. By six I gave up, and hitched back to Hazardsville.

Sam didn't show up the next day either, but none of us thought about calling the cops. Sam had gone off before, so we just went about our business and tried to sweat it out. By Monday noon the facts filtered down to us.

I was pulling Sam's tractor around the back of the barn, when Bobby called me. He was Ruby's husband, and not a bad guy for a boss. "Hollis!" I jumped down and waited for Bobby to cross through the dirt. It was a stinking hot day when all you could do would be dream about fishing or wish you was dead.

"I'm going on up to Springfield," Bobby said. "You wanna come along?" Bobby was a good ole boy too, with a slight hump on his back.

"Do I look like I want to go somewhere?" I asked him.

Bobby, who was about fifty years old and kept his hair cut short, took off his red bandanna and dipped it into the trough. He wrung it out. Some of the real old-timers used to wear wet cabbage leaves on their heads. "I just thought that you would want to fetch Sam with me." He didn't look at me. He kept his head bent toward the ground and dabbed at the back of his neck with the wet bandanna.

"Where is he?"

"Sam's dead," he said. With his boot he drew a tiny circle in the sand.

"Dead?"

Bobby nodded. He had been Sam's friend a long time, had known him a lot longer than I had known him.

"How do you know?" I asked him.

"The cops called. He shot himself. It's in the paper, if you want it. Ruby's got the paper back in the house." Bobby talked real soft-like, not raising his voice, not looking me in the face. I reached down and took some water out of the trough. I didn't feel like drinking. I just felt like scooping some water from the trough and allowing it to fall through my fingers.

"Shot himself?"

"Yeah."

I didn't bother to wash. We climbed into Bobby's pick-up, and Bobby told me the story. Sam had been with his girlfriend up in Springfield, and he had shot her. He had put it all in a note saying that he and the girl had been drinking, and that his rifle had gone off accidentally, sending a bullet through the girl's face. When Sam realized what he had done, he wrote out his farewell note and put the rifle into his mouth.

"When did they find him?" I asked.

"Early this morning. The girl was jailbait."

"They must have smelled something awful," I said. "In this heat."

"Damn it!" Bobby said, turning onto the highway. "What a damn fool thing to do!"

We drove for a while. "Let's go down by the river," I suggested. "I want to wash off." I was sweating like a pig.

"Forget it," Bobby said. "I'll buy you a six-pack on the way back."

# THE BLACK MESSIAH CAPE

Whatever Barney thought about it, Al called it The Black Messiah Cape, for today, tomorrow, sometime the Black Messiah would come, a Messiah from darkest Africa, strutting with natural rhythm and flashing a mouthful of pearly whites, so that when He smiled, sinners would rush out of their homes, throw themselves into the streets, and beg for forgiveness.

Neither Barney nor Al, however, could believe whole-heartedly in the concept of a Black Messiah, for always, out of somewhere, doubt would creep in, though the billboard at the corner of Rogers and Lattimore, six blocks from the Palace Theater where they both worked, six cold blocks on a winter's night, proclaimed: THUS SAITH THE LORD: BEHOLD I WILL RISE UP AGAINST BABYLON, AND AGAINST THEM THAT DWELL IN THE MIDST OF THEM THAT RISE UP AGAINST ME, A DESTROYING WIND. In fact, Al himself had observed that a destroying wind of sorts had already wreaked havoc upon the sign. Wind and rain had already obliterated many of the letters. Still, the message might be decoded if any observer, neutral or impassioned, had studied it long enough, and since Al passed the sign every night to and from his work, he had plenty of time to read it, to study it, and to pass his observations on to Barney.

But what did Barney know anyway, except that the picture of the white Messiah, dangling precariously on the edges of the billboard, was the only white man allowed in niggertown after dark, and the billboard marked a most visible boundary between hostile sections of town. Besides, what did Barney care about? He was always too busy tossing popcorn, counting tickets, jotting down seven-digit numbers in the ticket log, or eyeing the girls as they emerged from the ladies' room. Barney had even pointed out a peephole he had found to the bathroom. But when Al was given the cape to wear, Barney wasn't so free with his favors anymore.

Barney couldn't wear the cape because he was the ticket taker and not the head usher. Only the head usher, according to the mimeographed rule-sheet issued by the manager, could wear the cape, and so Al wore it three nights a week and twice on Sundays. On Sunday evenings he would stand on the sidewalk, waving a long flashlight and reminding the patrons to get in line for the next show. Most of the time, however, there weren't that many patrons, for the Baptist church had made a big fuss about showing films on Sunday.

"Al, how long have you been here?" Barney asked as he took a stack of popcorn boxes out of the closet. Folded flat, the boxes made a compact stack of red-and-white stripes on the edge of the refreshment counter.

"Three years." Al turned away. He was ashamed of the answer.

"I've been here five years. Five years today," Barney bragged.

"Maybe you'll die here."

"You wish."

"Why should I wish it? But if I got to die somewhere, what's wrong with here?"

Barney counted the boxes but didn't answer. A small, squat man with a few gray hairs on his head, he didn't enjoy arguing with Al. Al was still in high school, and Barney felt he still liked to show off. The irony of his last remark grated on Barney's nerves.

"Sure," Al continued. "Sure, you'll work for the Palace all your life, and then you'll die while taking tickets for *Gone with the Wind.*

The eighteenth re-run of *Gone with the Wind*, and as Scarlet O'Hara beats her horse to death, you're going to come down with a heart attack, and it's going to get you all sorts of national attention. They'll even fly in Darryl F. Zanuck and Leslie Howard and God knows who else, and they'll make a big speech over you, while you're lying on the carpet, foam coming out of your teeth; and at the end of the speeches, they'll carry you upstairs to the projectionist, and Ned Davis'll stuff you in a can of film and ship you back to Hollywood, where you'll be immortalized in a wax museum."

"Like hell they will."

"Like hell they won't."

"Besides, Leslie Howard's dead. You don't know nothing about the movies. You talk all the time how you're going to be a big-time actor, and you don't know nothing about acting. You couldn't fool a wart off a gnat's tail." Barney's head bobbed up and down as he filled a few of the popcorn boxes.

Al crossed behind the counter. "I can fool you, can't I?" He closed his right hand around the flashlight and gave Barney a friendly punch in the arm. Barney hit back, spilling some popcorn on the rug. Al was tall, skinny, with ribs that showed–a high school punk that Barney wasn't afraid of. Besides, it was horseplay. He and Al had engaged in it for the last three years.

"Can't you see I'm busy?" Barney wailed. "Now look what you made me do?"

"You're always busy." Al replied with another hit.

"Stop it, willya."

"Stop what?"

"Mr. Morganthal is coming!"

"Like hell he is."

"You're going to break your goddamn flashlight," Barney said, pulling away. "And I'm not going to buy you another one."

"And I'm not going to buy you another one," Al mimicked.

"Just look at yourself. That goddamn cape of yours hasn't been washed in a week." Barney regained his tone of authority.

"How can you tell? It's black. The dirt don't show."

"And you ain't been washed in a week either, I bet."

Barney, with official bearing, grabbed the hem of Al's cape and held it up to the light. The black velvet was edged with a thin red stripe. Barney ran his thumb over the edge of it. He found a snag. "Look, you dumb nigger, it's starting to rip. Mr. Morganthal paid good money for this cape, and you don't even know how to take care of it."

"Keep your nigger hands off it." Al brushed Barney's hand away from the cape. "You're the one who did it."

"Like hell I did!"

"That's where you hit me with your ring."

"It's your cape. I didn't do nothing to it."

Al retreated from Barney's grasp and pulled the cape to his body. "Well, don't worry your wooly head about it. I'll get my mother to mend it."

"You can't take it home." Barney plugged in the candy machine and turned on the lights over the red-and-white boxes. "It's against the rules."

"It's against the rules," Al mimicked. Al could mimic everybody, including Fra Morganthal, the manager. "I bet after ten years here you know all the rules."

"It's only been five, you wise-ass. Besides, that cape has to be mended by a professional. Mr. Morganthal don't want no dumb nigger like you walking home with his cape."

"Sah, sah, you know all the rules. Yes, sah. Let me shuffle for you, sah."

"Shut your dumb mouth because you don't know what you're talking about—as usual." Barney removed a clipboard from beneath the counter and consulted with the mimeographed sheet. "Suppose you took that cape home and you got sick," he continued, matter-of-factly, "and then Joshua or Michael showed up to take your place. Neither of them would have a cape to wear because you had it at home. Now whose ass would Mr. Morganthal be down on. He wouldn't just be down on you, let me tell you that. He'd be on your ass and he'd be on my ass. So I don't even want you to go around talking about taking that thing home. Here, you want to see the rules?" Barney held up the clipboard.

"Don't tell me what to do," Al said quietly. I'll wear the goddamn cape to graduation, if I want to."

"You just do that, honey," Barney said, dragging out a cardboard box from where the cartons of the soft-drink syrup were stored. "I hope I live so long to see you graduate. From what I hear, your high school's thinking about giving you a permanent locker, so you'll have a place to store your books for the rest of your life." Barney poured the carton of syrup into the Coke machine and replaced the top.

In front of the counter now, silhouetted by two rows of fluorescent tubes—the lights of the candy counter–, Al stretched out his arms, spreading his cape to its full length—the famous black count poised upon the steps of a spacious, but decaying mansion.

The final reel of film flashed to its end at five minutes after twelve. By a quarter to one, Al was on the street with the Messiah cape rolled under his sweater.

If anyone had asked him, Barney would have sworn up and down that the cape was hanging in the closet where it belonged, for he himself had watched Al hang it up. That was Al's idea. He wanted Barney to be certain that the cape was in the closet. As soon as Barney's back was turned, Barney applying his five-year-old skills to the counting of tickets, Al had lifted the cape from its hanger, rolled it into a tight ball, and slipped it under his sweater. He pressed the cape tightly to his right side and made a quick exit to the street, leaving Barney alone with a shoe box of torn tickets. Al had one other thing in his favor, for the manager had no reason to suspect that anything was wrong. Fra Morganthal had called the theater earlier in the evening, and Barney (by his own admission to Al) had forgotten to mention the tear in the cape. Apparently Barney hadn't felt the necessity to call Mr. Morganthal back, especially since Barney himself could be held partially responsible for tearing it.

But this was the part of the job that Al hated most – the long walk home after the final show. Sometimes he was lucky enough to hitch rides with friends who attended the films, but usually his friends had dates with them, or they were too busy to wait around for him. Besides, on Saturday night most of his friends were at the high school football game.

Al did have some money for a car of his own, but his mother was after him to save the money for college. That was a laugh all right, Al thought, but at least he had filled out an application for Florida A&M, for whatever that was worth. His only decent subjects were shop, gym, and something called "oral interpretation." Oral interpretation was the best of the lot because he could get up on the stage in front of everyone and pretend to be somebody he wasn't. His teacher suggested that he interpret something from *Inherit the Wind* or from *Green Pastures*, which showed what kind of a sap she was. Imagine thinking that *Green Pastures* was even worth reading. The very thought of it made Al bristle with anger.

Three blocks from the Palace, Al reached under his sweater and brought forth the cape, carefully unrolling it and trying to brush the wrinkles out. One look at all those wrinkles, Al thought, and Morganthal would collapse to the floor and foam at the mouth. Al checked the cape closely to make certain that the tear hadn't grown larger.

Renewed by his new sense of power, by a sense of the illicit, Al tied the cape about his narrow shoulders. He increased his stride and gave a short leap into the air. The streets were deserted ,so there was no fear of being seen by anybody. Suppose anybody did see him? What difference could it make? By day he was only a mild-mannered reporter working for a great metropolitan newspaper, but by night–ah, by night!–here was a different story. He was Super Nigger. Faster than a speeding locomotive, able to leap tall buildings in a single bound. Was it a bird? Was it a plane? No, it was Super Nigger, the Black Messiah come again, ready to stop silver bullets, bend steel with his bare hands, and circle the globe in thirteen seconds flat. The entire white world sat in fear that he would rise up against Babylon.

THUS SAITH THE LORD: BEHOLD I WILL RISE UP AGAINST BABYLON, AND AGAINST THEM THAT DWELL IN THE MIDST OF THEM THAT RISE UP AGAINST ME, A DESTROYING WIND.

In front of the battered billboard, its message sponsored jointly by the Calvary Baptist Church and the National Conference of Southern Christians, Al stretched forth his arms in the moonlight, displaying his cape at its full width. Deepening his voice, giving full projection the way his oral 'terp teacher suggested, he recited the board's message with ominous overtones. THUS, SAITH THE LORD: BEHOLD I WILL RISE UP AGAINST BABYLON, AND AGAINST THEM THAT DWELL IN THE MIDST OF THEM THAT RISE UP AGAINST ME, A DESTROYING WIND. He repeated the passage, repeated it and repeated it, until he had it down pat, until it mesmerized him slightly, led him to the brink of the darkened world and then back again. Al stopped. A noise from behind the billboard startled him.

"Who's there?" Al reached for the switchblade in his pocket. He carried the knife with him, always carried it with him ever since that night a carload of white boys tried to drag him and his date into an abandoned car. He wasn't going to let anybody try that again. "Come out from behind there," Al called, looking around him. It was not a safe hour to be walking through the white neighborhood that bordered niggertown, and Al didn't want to be caught in a trap. No answer came. "All right, you're going to be sorry if I have to come get you."

"Leave me alone. I ain't doing nothing," the voice said. Al relaxed slightly as the voice was the voice of a child. The torn picture of Christ rippled in the wind.

"Let me see you," Al commanded, gripping the knife, waiting for a possible trap.

"No. I ain't doing nothing." The voice began to cry. Al bent down and peered beneath the sign. A boy of nine or ten was lying on the ground with a blanket over him.

"What are you doing? Camping out?" Al asked, feeling more

confident, yet still puzzled by the presence of a white boy lying alone in Lattimore Field. "Where are your friends?"

"I ain't got no friends."

Al sensed the possibility of a trap, but he ducked under the billboard and stood up next to the boy. "So what are you doing here?" Al spread his legs apart, carefully distributing his weight, just in case.

"Nothing. I'm tired." The boy wiped his nose with his hands.

"What are you doing out so late? Does anybody know you're out here?" Al tossed the switchblade back and forth between his hands, thinking that maybe the presence of the knife would scare the boy. Shit, if it were some black boy out here and some white boys came upon him, there would be no telling what would happen.

"Nothing. I'm tired," the boy repeated, not even bothering to sit up.

Al looked at the kid. It was obvious from the smudges on the boy's face that he had been crying. Probably just one of the trashy kids living nearby, Al concluded. "Why don't you go home before you get into trouble? You don't belong here, don't you know that? Don't you know what happens to white boys here?"

The boy didn't say anything, but just lay there staring up at Al.

Al looked at the boy, looked him straight in the eye and pointed the blade of the knife at him. "Why don't you go home?" he suggested.

"'Cause."

"'Cause why?"

"'Cause I don't want to, that's why."

The boy's hair seemed blonde in the moonlight, and he didn't seem to have much on under the blanket, for Al could see his bare shoulders and arms. Brave little kid, thought Al. "Aren't you chilly out here with just one blanket?"

"No." Al could sense that the boy was lying. Al spat out of the side of his mouth just to show that he was tough, and then, deciding it wasn't a trap, pushed the knife back into the pocket of his usher's black pants. The kid was probably running away from home, Al thought, but he didn't even know enough to start a fire.

"Tell me where you live and I'll take you home," Al promised.

"I don't wanna go home." The kid had collected a pile of papers, wood, tin cans, and newspapers, and had even dug a little hole to put the stuff in, but there was still no fire. "You got some matches?" the boy asked.

Stupid kid, Al thought, running away without bringing any matches, and then running right into niggertown at that. Al kicked at the small pile of trash, attempting to straighten it with his foot. The papers were damp, and none of the stuff would have made a halfway decent fire. There was certainly no Boy Scout under that blanket. Al walked a few yards away, surveying the stretch of dirt and broken glass behind the billboard. Someone had dumped stacks of newspapers into the field, but most of the papers seemed soaked through from the rain. Al went through the piles carefully, attempting to find some dry ones. He carried a couple of sheets back to the boy.

"What's your name?" Al asked.

"Joel."

"Joel." Al spread the sheets over the single blanket. The blanket had holes in it, and through the holes Al could see the boy's white legs. "You can use dry newspapers if you get cold. Paper can keep you warm."

"What's your name?"

"Me?" Al paused dramatically and fingered the folds in his cape. "Me. I don't have one," he announced. He stood still, waiting to see the effect of his pronouncement.

"Then I don't have no name either," Joel said.

"Don't you know enough not to take your shoes off," Al answered angrily, attempting to cover his immense disappointment. "You might have to make a fast getaway and then where will you be?" Al held a pathetic shoe up to the moon, a white tennis sneaker with its laces broken.

"Put it down," Joel said.

"Look, I'm going to take you home," Al said, "before somebody sees you. There's all kinds of gangs roaming around here looking for trouble. A kid like you they'd eat for supper."

"No," Joel said, "I ain't scared."

"Like hell you ain't," Al said, picking up on Barney's phrase.

"Leave me alone," Joel whined.

"Don't tell me what to do," Al exploded. "I've got as much right to be here as you do. More right, in fact. Do you know who I am?" Al squatted down, pushing his face close to Joel's face. "Do you know who I am?"

"No," Joel answered, frightened by Al's outburst of temper.

"Do you see what I'm wearing? Do you know why I go around wearing this cape?"

Joel stared back in horror.

"I'm the Black Messiah, that's who I am. The Black Messiah," Al said loudly, shouting into the boy's face, stretching out the final word, breaking it into syllables and laying on it the final emphasis of Annunciation. Joel's mouth fell open, but he didn't say anything. "You know what a Messiah is, don't you?" Al asked.

Joel stared for an ungodly time. At last he confessed. "I forget," he stammered, turning away form the macabre figure who loomed over him in the moonlight.

"Don't you understand, stupid?" Al continued with great vehemence. "Christ has risen. Jesus Christ has come. The Black Messiah has returned."

Joel's head jerked back in a startled gesture, as if it were involuntarily coming loose at the neck, as if the jaw had been on a loose hinge, and although he struggled to fight back the tears, he began to cry.

"You're a real crybaby, aren't you?" Al taunted, taking fiendish pleasure in the power that had been given unto him. "What are you crying for?" he demanded. "What are you crying for? There's nothing to be afraid of. There's nothing to be scared of."

Joel twisted his skinny arms and legs around the blanket. "Oh.... Oh," he moaned, his body almost out of control.

The sight of the boy thrashing about upon the ground caused Al to freeze. He softened his voice to quiet the boy's torment. "I'm here. Don't you understand? I'm here." Al stretched forth his arms in a gesture of openness and pity, a regal gesture he had copied from one of the actors in the high school play. "I'm here. Everything's all right."

Joel lay resting, gasping for his breath.

"What's wrong with you?" Al asked. "Are you all right?"

Joel opened his eyes. "My momma says that when Jesus comes, we're all going to die. I don't want to die."

The simplicity of the recital stunned Al. On one hand, he enjoyed the masquerade, and, on the other, he felt ashamed, frightened that he struck some wound, triggered some disease. He closed his right hand into a fist and then slowly extended his forefinger. "You're not going to die," he said matter-of-factly. "As long as I'm here you're not going to die." The softness of the reply soothed Joel's nerves.

Al stood up and raised his arms to a deserted world. "I've come to bring you home. The Black Messiah has come to lead a lost lamb back to the fold." Al's mind raced for some fancy rhetoric, for a speech or two from *Green Pastures*. He turned back to Joel. "After all, you can't sleep out here all night, can you?" he added as an afterthought.

Joel pulled the blanket closer to his face, his mouth biting on the coarse material. At last he raised his head. "But I don't wanna go home," he pleaded. "I don't wanna never go home."

"Why?"

"'Cause."

"'Cause ain't an answer."

Joel didn't reply, but lay there with his wet eyes opened, not really crying, not really looking. His mother had told him about the Messiah, about Jesus on the cross. And the Messiah was everywhere, but now he was here, and now he was black, and Joel kept thinking how the dead were going to rise up out of their graves and go straight to heaven, where everybody was happy. Perhaps he himself would rise into the sky, float up and up and up, but then only if the Messiah wanted him to.

"You want me to read your mind?" Al was impatient for an answer why this skinny white boy would be sleeping out under a billboard at night. "I can, you know. I can tell you what you're thinking about." Holy Jesus, if the oral 'terp teacher were only here now, Al thought, what a fit she'd have. Her and her *Green Pastures* slop. He'd show her how to act, all right. She'd have to give him an A for the course. Maybe someday his name would be up in the lights, and Barney would shit a cupcake. Al Farnung, Jr., as the Black Messiah, produced by Darryl F. Zanuck, and costarring Leslie Howard as the walking dead. And Barney would have to put his name up in front of the theater, and Fra Morganthal might even ask him for his autograph, and he'd answer, 'No siree, Bob,' because he wouldn't even let him take home the Messiah cape when he wanted to, no matter if nobody was wearing it or not. Al savored the dream for a long time. At last he said, "If Jesus asks you a question, you've got to answer it. Don't you know that? You can't say no to Jesus."

Joel blinked his eyes. "He's beating up my mother."

"Who's beating up your mother?" Super Nigger to the rescue, Al thought, as his heart quickened, and he envisioned his cape in a new context.

Joel didn't say anything. It seemed to bother him not to know whether this Black Messiah was really the same Jesus or just a different one.

"Who's beating up your mother?" Al repeated quietly.

"My step-father."

"Oh."

"He's not my real father. He's my step-father," Joe said as if it explained everything.

Al noticed the dirt on the hem of the cape and winced. It was one thing to ask his mother to sew a small tear in the material, but it was another to ask her to wash it. He didn't know whether he could wash velvet or not, and the thought of it shrinking brought him sadistic pleasure. Morganthal would scream bloody murder at him.

"Why? You can tell me."

"I don't know. They fight."

Screw the cape, Al thought. He kneeled down beside the boy and placed his left hand on the boy's curly blond hair. His right hand touched the hard dirt of Lattimore Field. "Now listen to me, Joel. I want to tell you something and I want you to do exactly as I say."

Joel nodded, as if in a trance. Al's hand felt warm on his forehead.

"I want you to put on your shoes and follow me. I want you to get up and walk home with me. I'm going to take you home. Get up, you're going home."

Joel sat up and began putting on his shoes. His actions were slow, mechanical. He wore only a pair of shorts cut from an old pair of dungarees.

"This your blanket?" Al asked.

"Yeah."

"You find it?"

"Naah. I brought it from home."

Al looked at the moon hanging blankly over niggertown. "It must be around one-thirty," he said.

"So?"

"So?"

Joel finished with his shoes, leaving the knotted laces on one untied. He stood up, pulling the blanket with him.

Al stood up and led the way under the billboard. "Where do you live?"

"Around the block," Joel answered, following under the sign, but being careful not to brush against the cape. "Can I touch it?"

"Touch what?"

"'The cape."

"No, you can't touch it," Al said gravely.

"Why not?"

"Because," Al answered.

"Because?"

"Yeah, just because," he said.

As they left the lot, Joel said, "You don't look like Jesus."

"And what does Jesus look like?" Al demanded.

"His picture's on the sign back there. Didn't you see it? Jesus is a white man."

"I used to be white, but I ain't no more," Al explained. "Because I discovered that white is evil and I don't want to be that color no more. And I can be any color I want to be."

Al stayed in front of Joel and wouldn't let the boy catch up. "I can be any color I want to be, and I don't want to be white no more. That's why they call me the Black Messiah."

Joel quickened his pace. "What are you going to do to my step-father," he asked. His naked arms and chest were covered with goose-bumps because the blankets kept slipping away from him.

"What do you mean, what am I going to do to him?"

If anyone had been looking out the window onto Rogers Street, he would have been greeted by the sight of two strangers, one in a cape, and the other in an army blanket, zigzagging between the shadows of the houses. An older person might have been reminded of the Black Legion out for a midnight mission, but nobody was up. At least nobody was up on Joel's block. The houses blinked dolefully under the damp burr of the street lights, though a couple of blocks away, the Ebony Tiger was still going full swing. Al and Joel could hear the songs of a faraway jukebox, and then the sounds of drums. Joel fell behind, then hurried to catch up again, staying two or three steps behind and always careful that the swaying cape did not touch his arms or legs.

"What do you mean, what am I going to do to him?" Al repeated.

"Can you change him into something?"

A tricycle on the edge of the road came out of nowhere, and Al nearly tripped over it. He turned it over with a clatter. "Look, I'm just bringing you home. I don't want to get messed up in nothing." Al knew that he could make Joel do anything he wanted him to do, even murder for him if he asked it, and the feeling excited him.

"Can you walk on water?" Joel asked nervously.

"I can walk on nails if I want to, but those are magician's tricks. Don't you understand? I'm the Messiah, not a magician. God doesn't want me to change people into things or to walk on water."

"Jesus walked on water." Joe halted in front of a light-colored house. Either yellow or white or light green. In the moonlight it looked white. The screen door was slightly ajar, and a light burned in the kitchen. The steps and the porch were deserted. To the rear of the porch, near the screen door, a sweet potato plant stood in a large white pot.

"This is my house here," Joel said when he saw that Al hadn't stopped.

Al stopped and glared at the house. "I know," he said. "I know where you live. I know everything."

"Can you walk on water?"

"I told you."

"Will you?"

"No, I won't. Now look," Al said. "It's getting late. I'm tired. I've put in a hard day already. If I hadn't come along, some gang would be beating up on you right now. Cutting you up and eating you for supper. So go in and be thankful for what you've got. You can't have everything."

Joel sat on the steps and stubbornly pulled his knees up to his chin. With the soiled blanket wrapped around him, he resembled not so much a runaway as a refugee in a newsreel–a bombed-out child hiding from a war.

"You going in with me?"

"Why should I go in with you?"

Joel started to cry.

"Stop it, willya? There's no sense thinking about it. We've all got to suffer. You've got to suffer for me; you've got to pay for your sins with tears. Everybody suffers for Jesus; you know that. Everybody knows that. Even the Jews suffer for Jesus. That's what being religious means."

Joel wiped his nose with his arm.

Al sat down on the steps. "You suffer for me," he said, "and then you'll go to heaven. In heaven, you'll be happy. Everybody's happy in heaven." Al peered into Joel's eyes. "You know what a parable is?"

"No."

'Then forget it. I was going to tell you a parable, but there's no sense telling you one, when you don't even know what it is."

"Tell me."

"No." Al made the sign of the cross with his right hand, motioning slowly in the air. "I bless you in the name of the Father and the Son and the Holy Ghost. Amen."

"Jesus could walk on water," Joel exclaimed.

"That's because people believed in Him. They believed in the Messiah. They even knew what the parables were."

"I believe in the Messiah."

"Believe in me," Al cried forcefully. "Believe in me. Say you believe in me."

Joel stared into the depths of the cape with round believing eyes.

"Believe in me." Al intensified his efforts. "Say you believe in me."

"I believe in you," Joel mumbled, the cape moving closer to his head.

"Believe in me," Al shouted.

Joel's head jerked back, and a bit of spittle appeared at the corners of his mouth. Al awkwardly reached out to grab him.

Joel's left leg shook uncontrollably, and his breath came in spurts. "Joel, stop it, willya?" He grabbed Joel by the shoulders and shook him. "I didn't mean nothing by it. You can believe in anybody you want to." He placed his face near Joel's. "Christ, I didn't mean nothing by it. Can't you understand? You're just a dumb little kid to let somebody frighten you like that." Al gathered Joel into his arms, carried him up the stairs, and placed him on the porch. His impulse was to leave him there, leave him between the overturned wooden chair and the remnants of the plant in the white pot. As Al bent over Joel, adjusting the blanket and making sure Joel was still breathing, a woman appeared in the doorway, a heavy woman in a pink slip. She pushed the screen door open. It scraped against the porch until it stopped against Joel's naked leg.

"You the one raising the ruckus, boy?" she said, holding the door, holding on to it with one unsteady hand, while the other groped for a light switch on the inside wall. The straps of her slip had fallen from her shoulders, and Al stared with fascination and embarrassment.

"I...I...found your son, ma'am," Al managed to stammer through the darkness.

The woman stood silhouetted against the lit hallway, the light shining through her slip. Al tried to look away from the woman's large breasts, but he couldn't. He was too taken with fear and desire.

"What...what did you say, boy?" The woman brushed her hair away from her eyes, black hair that tumbled to her shoulders. It was obvious to Al, obvious from the unsteady stance at the door, her fumblings with the light switch, that the woman had been drinking. "You heard me. You the one raising the ruckus?"

A man's voice boomed above behind her, perhaps from upstairs. "Cora, what the hell is going on down there?"

A naked light bulb illuminated the porch.

"Cora, get your fat ass up here."

Al gulped. "I found your son, ma'am.... He was out sleeping in the field." The glare from the naked light momentarily hurt Al's eyes, but through the screen he saw that Cora had a shiner. Her jaw was swollen, and her left eye was black and blue. Cora pressed her forehead against the screen. "Oh my gawd, my gawd!"

"CORA!"

"Shut your face. I'm coming!"

Al fingered the cape that hung down about him and felt foolish, a traveling magician strolling door to door in costume. "You know.... The field down at Lattimore and Rogers.... He was sleeping there."

Joel groaned in his sleep.

"Oh gawd, gawd, what's wrong with my boy?" Cora moaned, pressing herself against the screen.

"Nothing," Al lied. "Nothing. He's just sleeping that's all."

"Don't lie to me, boy. He's had another attack, hasn't he? Gawddammit, ain't I got enough troubles?"

"Cora, who you got down there with you?"

Al wondered why the man upstairs hadn't come down, but he was glad he hadn't.

"What do you want me to do?" Cora pleaded. "Can't you see that I can't do nothing about it?"

Al tried to stare at his shoes, but his glance kept returning to the woman's breasts. "Maybe you oughta to call a doctor?"

"For sleeping?" Cora kept her head pressed against the screen, looking down on her son. Joel stirred, slowly reviving. "I thought you said there was nothing wrong with him?"

"He might have caught a cold out in the field," Al said flatly.

"The doctor's already been here once tonight."

Seeing that Cora was in no condition to help, Al bent over the boy.

"You leave him alone," she cried. "Just who do you think you are, putting your hands all over my boy like that?"

"CORA, I'm going to come get you!"

"What did you do to my boy?" she wailed. "What did you niggers do to my boy?"

"I'll bring him in for you," Al said, his face burning. He gathered Joel into his arms.

"You leave him right there," Cora shrieked. "You leave him right there!" She made an abortive gesture of covering her breasts.

"But you can't leave him out here all night. He's hardly got anything on." Al's eyes flashed with anger. He could hear the man upstairs gagging and heaving.

Cora's elbows bent heavily on the crosspiece of the screen door as she held her head in her hands. In the distance, the music from the Ebony Tiger continued, distinct and unceasing. "Why do your kind come here raising a ruckus for this time of night?"

"Cora, you gotta help me." A black man, naked from the waist up and wearing a pair of blue pajama bottoms, appeared, kneeling on the top of the stairs. Al could see him grasping at the banister. Cora didn't answer him.

"What time is it? What time is it that you come around here waking everybody up for?" Cora shook her head back and forth in the light.

"Cora." The man's voice was hoarse from heaving. He pressed his face to the railing.

Cora mumbled into her palms. "Are you the one raising the ruckus? Why are you coming around here raising a ruckus?"

"Look Cora," Al said angrily.

"Don't get fresh with me!"

"I ain't getting fresh with you." The sense of power had returned to Al. "I'm just tired. I can't stand here all night holding your kid."

Joel's eyelids fluttered.

"Leave me be. Leave me be." She pushed her bulk closer to the wall so that Al could squeeze by. She averted her face because she was ashamed to let the stranger see her black eye. She still grasped the door, so Al had to squeeze through. Joel stirred in his arms. "Black Messiah," he muttered. "Black Messiah."

Cora turned to the man kneeling on the stairs, his nose protruding between the slats in the banister. "What's the boy saying?" the man asked.

"He's found Joel. He's bringing Joel home," she explained.

The man raised his chin. There were dry streaks of blood on his neck, fingernail scratches. "Tell him to stick him in the toilet."

"You black bastard!" Cora wailed. "You fucking sonofabitch!" Al looked at the woman and their eyes met in a profusion of embarrassment. She paused, lowering her head. "Don't listen to us. He don't mean nothing by it. He don't mean nothing by it. He's just joking, that's all…." Cora made a feeble wave of her hand. The other hand tightly clutched the crosspiece of the door. "It's just his idea of a joke," she apologized. "You know what I mean."

Al moved closer to the man on the stairs. His blue pajamas were soaked through, and his arms and chest were covered with sweat. Al's mouth felt dry, and the stench of the crowded hallway upset his stomach. "Where do you want me to put him?" he asked Cora.

"Why are you wearing that thing?" Cora asked. "I ain't seen nobody walking around here in a cape."

Al didn't answer. He placed Joel on a yellow hall-sofa that stood next to the staircase, next to a small table with a lamp on it.

"Whatja got that cape on for?" Cora repeated. "You see that? You see what he's wearing?"

Al attempted to adjust the blanket, but Joel sat straight up like someone in a trance. "Black Messiah, Momma. Black Messiah." He remained upright.

"What's the kid mumbling about now?" asked the man on the stairs.

"He must still think it's Halloween," Cora said laughing.

"Black Messiah," Joel repeated in his fever.

Al turned away from the child and faced Cora, who continued to giggle. "He's saying I'm the Black Messiah," he announced. His body tensed, and the veins in his neck stood out. "Can't you hear anything? He says I'm the Black Messiah." He lost control of his left leg, and it began shaking. He could feel his heart pounding. "Can't you understand anything!" he shouted. "I found your son dying, and I brought him home. I did. Nobody else did. And I'm the Black Messiah. That's who I am." Al walked with deliberate strides to the door, his head held high and the cape flaring behind him. A cold wind blew through the screen. "That's the trouble with you poor white trash and you dumb niggers. You don't understand. You don't understand anything." Al turned back to Joel, who sat stiffly on the sofa. There were tears in Al's eyes, and his body trembled. With his right hand he made a fist. His left went for the switchblade in his pocket.

Cora put her hand to her face and laughed aloud. "Oh lawdy, just listen to him. Some kook comes in here wearing a cape, and we're supposed to be washed in the blood of the lamb."

The man on the stairs attempted to stand up, but he sat back down again. "You just get your black ass out of here," he said feebly, trying to take command. "Get out of here and don't come back." He turned to his wife. "Cora, you cover yourself up."

"And to think we got the Black Messiah here!" Cora laughed.

"You just don't understand," Al exclaimed. "You just don't understand anything at all." Al pushed Cora's arm away from the door.

"I wish I had a cape like that. A cape like that to swish around in."

"Cora, cover yourself up," the man ordered.

Al glanced about in confusion, angry at himself, humiliated at his loss of dignity. Cora lowered her bulk to her knees, allowing her pink slip to climb up her thighs. "Oh yes, cover up," she mimicked, "cuz we have the Black Messiah here." She lifted her head in mock prayer, the light from the wooden table adding purple shades to her black and blue contusions. "Oh, Lawd, forgive us cuz we have all sinned. Wash us in the blood of the lamb."

"That's not my father," Joel said.

"Fools! Can't you see nothing?" Al crossed to the porch, allowing the screen-door to bang behind him. He turned and stared at the kneeling woman. Through her pink slip he could see her black underwear and the wide rolls of flesh. He desired her, desired her, and hated that in himself. "You better get Joel to a doctor," he cried.

"I done told you that the doctor has already been here once tonight." Cora stopped laughing and brushed the stringy hair away from her eyes. "And what are you staring at?" she demanded, remembering her bruised face, her dishevelled clothing.

"Nothing."

"Damn right. Nothing. There's nothing here for you," she laughed.

Al's cheeks burned. "Bitch!" He ran down the stairs with his cape flying behind him.

"And just don't come back here," Cora screamed from her

knees. "You just mind your own business, hear."

"Cora, cover up," the man pleaded.

"You just mind your own business, hear," Cora screamed at Al. "The next time you see my son lying in some field, you just let him be. You let him be, you hear? You keep out of where you don't belong. I don't want him frightened by no jigaboo."

Al ran past the overturned tricycle, and then slowed. Goddamn them anyway, he thought. Just who do they think they are?

At the end of the block, he turned toward Lattimore Field and automatically began untying the cape, loosening the black bow that held it to his neck, but when he caught his breath and noticed what he was doing, he tied the cord tighter, leaving the cape on. What the hell! he said to himself. What the hell difference does it make anyway? No matter what I do, Barney's going to yell his head off anyway.

# THE MAN WHO OWNED THE PALACE

My father is a barber, and my mother works at one of the local dress shops, so I'm in town all the time, and I know what's going on. I just don't come in once a week like some of my friends. That's why when the Palace reopened, I took more interest in it than most people. Television is all right, but not when you have to watch it with your parents, especially when your father falls asleep and snores so loud that you can hardly hear what's coming off.

Anyway, the Palace used to be a movie theater when my father was a boy, and he went there to see Chaplin and William S. Hart and all those other guys. He used to like going to the movies, but when he got married, he got out of the habit, and now he hardly ever goes. I guess he hasn't seen a movie in four or five years, not counting the one we halfway seen. My mother likes movies a lot, but mostly she's tired after work, and so she watches them on television. New movies aren't very good, she says. Of course she belongs to another generation.

As I was saying, the Palace used to be a movie theater when my father was a boy. Then it closed for the longest time. It was closed almost all the time I was growing up, and a closed movie theater gives me the goose bumps. Outside there are huge red letters announcing a movie that's been there and one that's not coming again. It's strange when people are too lazy to even take down the letters. When I was about six or seven, though, somebody opened it up again, but only at night. The first show was around seven, and the last show at nine, and it cost only ten cents to get in—for children, that is. I saw some great films there, but I guess I like best the movie where a parrot and Donald Duck and some other animals go to South America. There were cartoon figures and live people in it, and it was really good. I saw a lot of movies there, but then it closed down again. It was made into a Western Auto Store for a while, until that business moved across the street. And then nothing. For a while someone thought that the Baptist Church would take it over, but the congregation vetoed the idea. Finally, it was left alone.

And so the Palace was closed most of the time when I really needed it because when I started dating there was nowhere to go except to our high school's football games, which were okay, but then the girls usually fell for the football players instead of for me. But right after my eighteenth birthday, Fra Morganthal decided to re-open the Palace. I had known Mr. Morganthal briefly before, for he came to my father for his haircuts and because he had a strange reputation around town.

Mr. Morganthal had come to Gaffney to take care of his widowed sister. She had suffered a stroke, and he had come down from New York to be with her. They kept to themselves most of the time, and when she died about six months later, not too many people went to the funeral. Also, he wore a beard, which didn't help him out none. My father was always after him to shave it off, but he never would, and my mother would say that he "looked like the very devil with that beard on," and that she "wouldn't trust no man who don't show his face."

The beard wasn't the main thing, though. The main thing was that Mr. Morganthal never went to church and that, although he was rich, he refused to help the church out in any way. In fact, he didn't do much of anything. Usually he spent his days walking around the town or reading in the public library. About a few months before he took over the Palace, Fredericka Thompson, one of the high school girls who worked at the library, got into trouble, so to speak, and some of the women said that it was Mr. Morganthal's doing, until a boy home from the Navy came forward to marry her. Fredericka never said nothing, and nothing was ever really proved one way or the other. Fredericka and her husband just moved away.

Maybe I haven't told you, but I used to go to the library a lot myself because I liked reading and because I wanted to be a writer in the worst way, so I was one of the few persons who got to know Mr. Morganthal. When I say that I got to know him, I don't mean to say that we were friends, but that he got to know me by name. We used to sit in front of the library and talk, waiting for Mrs. Hendrix to open the doors.

I was one of the persons Mr. Morganthal asked about the Palace Theater. "Where do you go to see a movie around here?" he asked me one day, taking a cigar out of his shirt pocket and sitting down on the library steps. He had a couple of books with him, and he set the books down beside him. I guess they were overdue because he had a two-dollar bill sticking out of the pages.

"I don't know," I told him. "I don't go too often. Sometimes me and my friends go up to the Star-Lite. That's the drive-in, but that's a long ways away."

"How far?" He wiped his brow with a silk handkerchief. I never saw anybody who sweat as much as Mr. Morganthal. He had been raised in the North, so he wasn't used to the heat.

"I think it's about time we brought some culture to this town," hesaid. " I've decided to open a movie theater."

"That would be great. I get a little tired having to go to the Baptist Church all the time to see movies. Did you run a movie theater in New York?"

"No. But I thought about it several times. It's a great city, but it probably doesn't need another movie theater."

"I guess when I join the Army I'll get to see it," I told him. I hadn't even told my parents that I was thinking of joining the army.

"When my sister was sick," Mr. Morganthal said, "I often

wishedfor a movie to go to. Gaffney needs one."

"A movie theater would be great, but I don't see how you're going to make much money from it."

"Oh, I'll  do all right I guess." He smiled at me. I had never seen him smile before and some of his teeth were capped with gold. I had notived that before, but now I really noticed it, if you know what I mean.

"You'll probably get your biggest crowds on Friday and Saturday,"I told him, just to let him know I had a head for business. "That's when everybody comes to town."

"Well, I won't be able to run the theater myself," he replied, asif he were reading my mind.

I was going to tell him I knew how to thread a projector, because I had taken an audio-visual course so I could help teachers show films in their classes, but then he said, "I want you to be my head usher. That is if, if you want to work for me."

"You mean it?"

"Of course I mean it. Also, I need somebody who can operate a 35-mm projector. Who was the projectionist before the theater closed down?"

"I can't remember exactly, but I think it was Ned Davis. Do you want me to ask him for you?"

"No, I'll take care of it myself. Why don't you see if some of your friends want to be ushers?"

"How many will you need?"

"About six, I guess."

"Six? The Palace never even had one before."

"But this is the new Palace. We're going to do it up right. Son, it's going to be great!"

As soon as my friends at school heard that I was able to get them a job ushering at the Palace, I became the most popular student in history. With my own parents, however, it was a different story.

"You're not going to work for Mr. Morganthal, and that's all there is to it," my mother told me. "Your father needs you to sweep out the store and run errands for him. Let one of your friends—let Bobby Hendrix—be the head usher. We're not going to have you working on school nights."

"But I'm almost out of school. I'm going to be graduating soon, and this will be a good job in the summer. It'll give me something to do before going into the army." The word *army* usually shattered my mother's arguments, but she tried not to let her feelings show.

"You're not going to do it. We have no idea what kind of man Mr. Morganthal is. He doesn't go to church. He refuses to shave his beard. Besides, I hear he uses language that would—well, I don't even want to talk about it," said my mother.

"But he's a steady customer."

"He hardly says nothing to me," my father said. "Hardly get a 'morning' out of him. My other customers don't mind jawing with me, but he don't say nothing. Just sits there while I cut."

"But I like him," I said. "And besides he's going to pay me a dollar-and-a-half an hour."

"Oh my God!" my mother exclaimed. Never before in my life had I ever heard her use the Lord's name in vain, but she was only earning a dollar-and-a-quarter an hour at the dress shop.

"If you don't let me take the job, then you'll have to pay me a dollar-and-a-half an hour to sweep up the barbershop."

"Hell no, I ain't," said my father, getting out of his easy chair. "I can get some nigger to come in and sweep up for seventy-five cents an hour. A dollar-and-a-half an hour! Who's he trying to fool? He won't be able to keep the theater open a week if he pays those kind of wages."

"He's rich, and he wants to do something good for Gaffney."

"Well, if he wants to do some good," my father answered, "you tell him to pack up his theater and move it to Atlanta or someplace where they'll appreciate it. We got one drive-in around here, and that's enough, and they don't go around paying young kids a buck-and-a-half an hour."

It was the wages that really burned my parents, and it was

the wages that finally convinced them that I should work. "Just long enough to see if it will work out," my mother said. "If it don't work out, then you'll go to work in the furniture factory. Then you'll see what it's like to work for your living. It ain't like sweeping out the barbershop, let me tell you that."

So I became the head usher for the soon-to-be-opened Palace Theater, and I was Mr. Morganthal's right-hand man. At least I thought I was his right-hand man, although he hardly ever told me nothing. But I got Dale Jenkins, Bobby Hendrix, Matt Robinson, Harvey Slater, and Lance Wheeler to be ushers with me, and I got a job for Elizabeth Burns, one of my girl friends. She was going to sell tickets out front. So things were really shaping up. Even Ned Davis decided to move back into town and be the projectionist. He was getting paid twice as much as the other owner paid him. But Ned started strutting through town like the cat-of-the-walk, and the whites didn't like that too much.

Mr. Morganthal scheduled the grand opening of the Palace for the day after the high school graduation, and that also made it easier for me to take the job. But my mother was still angry about the dollar-and-a-half an hour, especially since Ned Davis, a common nigger, never had a high school education. Some of the merchants in town tried to talk with Mr. Morganthal about it, but he refused to lower his wages. He told them to mind their own businesses. After the meetings, there was some talk that the Klan would burn a cross on Davis' lawn if he dared to show up at the theaterr, but it didn't take place. I guess that's because the people in town were really hungry for motion pictures. And, though the merchants weren't happy about the wage scale, they knew the theater would bring more people back to town. The furniture people were especially happy because Mr. Morganthal had the Palace completely redecorated, from top to bottom. An entire new front was built, and at night the letters spelling out PALACE blinked on and off, first one at a time, then all together. It added a touch of class to the main street.

In addition to helping Mr. Morganthal in finding ushers and

ticket takers and girls to sell popcorn, I was also in charge of picking out the uniforms. Mr. Morganthal said not to worry about the expense, so I looked at his catalogues and picked out the fanciest uniforms they had—a dark blue uniform, with gold stripes down the sides and gold epaulets. The ushers would wear white gloves and carry a flashlight, and since I was the captain, I'd wear captain stripes on my left sleeve. Believe you me, I couldn't wait for the Palace to open.

Not everything was going smoothly, however, for I was well into my final weeks at school and was sweating over a passing grade in math, when a fresh debate broke out over the theater. It was May, and no ads had appeared in the Gaffney Bulletin, and everybody was curious about what movie Mr. Morganthal would open with. I myself hoped that it would be something in Technicolor, perhaps a spy film, but I was afraid to mention it. I figured he knew more about films than I did, so I didn't say anything. But when the first ad appeared, a full-page one with a photograph of Mr. Morganthal in front of his theater, there was no mention of the movie's name, only the fact that there would be a sneak preview for a specially invited audience on Saturday night, and that the Palace would open for regular business on Sunday morning.

It was the Sunday morning show that did it. As soon as the church leaders read that, they nearly burnt the theater to the ground. Phones of the church members were ringing twenty-four hours a day ,and my mother told me that a dollar-fifty an hour or no dollar-fifty an hour, that I would not be ushering on Sunday, and that I would be singing in the choir as usual. My other friends, except for Harvey Slater, whose parents were atheists, were in the same boat as I was, but when I told Mr. Morganthal, he said not to worry because he would hire a special Sunday staff. He went out and hired six blacks from out of town, at three dollars an hour, to work the Sunday showings. When I heard that, I nearly cried.

Next Sunday in church was almost like the Fourth of July. The Reverend Sayer spoke out against all those who dared to profane the Lord's Day, against all those who used the tools of the devil to lure children and adults away from the Bosom of the Lord. I liked the way he said "bosom" because he could hardly say it without a blush, though I myself had looked at Christ's picture closely and had never seen anything to blush about. The members of the City Council, though, took heed of Reverend Sayer's word and strengthened their Sunday laws. They served notice to Mr. Morganthal that it would be against the law to open his movie theater before one o'clock on a Sunday. Mr. Morganthal quietly informed them that he would take it all the way to the Supreme Court if necessary, since it was obviously unconstitutional to tell a man when he might open for business. Mr. Morganthal also demanded that since Sunday does not mean the same thing to all religions, that all stores be closed on Saturdays out of respect to the Jews. At which point, Mr. Farley, the mayor of Gaffney over the past six years, said Mr. Morganthal would burn in hell, and that the City Council would do everything in its power to keep the Palace from ever opening. Members of the KKK began to form plans to keep the Sunday staff from showing up.

"We'll be damned if we'll allow a movie theater to interfere with God's work," was how one of the Klan members put it to my father. "Can you imagine a nigger earning three dollars an hour just for standing there and watching a movie?" I wanted to answer him, but my father glared me down. He also had his razor strap nearby.

On Tuesday, the *Gaffney Bulletin* ran an editorial against Sunday movies and flatly told Mr. Morganthal that he couldn't use their paper for advertising. For a few days, Mr. Morganthal considered printing his own one-page advertisements and distributing them by mail, but he finally relented. He got back into the town's good graces by canceling the Sunday morning showing. He wrote a note of apology to the *Bulletin*, and everything settled back to normal again. I was slightly disappointed that the battle had been lost, but Mr. Morganthal said he was more worried about the lives of his staff than he was about losing face. Still, he refused to tell me about the movies he had booked, and I couldn't wait until Saturday night because I had never attended a sneak preview before.

The week before the grand opening of the Palace was a quiet one for me. Most of my exams were finished, and I was just waiting around to graduate. In the mornings I'd help Mr. Morganthal mail out engraved invitations to the grand opening; in the afternoons I would drive a rented car over to the bus station to pick up guests who were beginning to arrive from New York and Atlanta. I personally delivered invitations to the mayor, the members of the city council, and to the editor of the *Bulletin* just to show there were no hard feelings.

Naturally it didn't take too long for those invitations to become status symbols. Most of the families had tickets to our high school graduation, but not too many families had tickets to the opening. Since I was the head usher, I got two invitations, although my father, at first, didn't want to go. When he found out, however, that the mayor and members of the city council were invited, he changed his mind and decided to take his chance on the movie.

"What's the movie going to be?" my father asked.

I told him I didn't know. It was a surprise.

"Fine way to run a business," he snorted.

"He wants it to be a real surprise. It may be a new Elizabeth Taylor and Richard Burton movie."

"That hussy!" my mother said.

"But I don't know what the movie is," I told her.

I even asked Ned Davis, on the chance that he might have seen the film cans when they arrived, but he told me that Mr. Morganthal had picked up the films personally and was keeping them under lock and key at his home.

"Didn't he say nothing to you at all?"

"Nah, nothing," Ned said.

Saturday night couldn't arrive fast enough for me. I must have spent several hours on Friday and Saturday trying on my usher's uniform and pacing back and forth in front of the mirror, while my mother repeated, "Vanity, Edward, vanity. All is vanity." But on Saturday afternoon, when my mother came home early with a new dress and a permanent wave, I teased her with her own words. All my father did was grumble, "I don't care who's coming, I'd at least like to know what movie it is. Saturday night is a good television night."

I left the house early, around four o'clock. I had to pick up more persons at the bus station. What was even more important, however, was that Mr. Morganthal had chartered two busloads of people to come all the way from Atlanta. They had pulled into the parking lot of the Veranda, Gaffney's only hotel, and the whole town was buzzing because nothing like it had ever happened in its history. The mayor was walking around like a pigeon with his chest puffed out, as if the whole thing were his own idea. I had my uniform in the trunk of the car, and I was torn between putting it on early and taking a chance of getting it wrinkled, or waiting until the final few minutes, only to find that the zipper would be stuck. I was in such a fret that I even arranged for one of my friends to be nearby in case one of the ushers didn't show up. I also personally delivered the tickets to the ticket booth, although they weren't needed until Sunday afternoon.

On the front porch of the Veranda, I saw Mayor Farley having a long talk with Mr. Morganthal, and, as a result, the fire and police departments drove a large arc light up in front of the theater. The sky was going to be lit up just like a regular Hollywood premiere. In fact, there was a rumor that several movie stars were going to be on hand, although I doubted it. Even Mr. Morganthal couldn't convince them to come to Gaffney, Georgia.

At seven o'clock, Mr. Morganthal arrived at the theater, inspected the screen, the seats, the candy counter, and carried the film up into the projection booth. The film was in an unmarked case, so I couldn't see the title. I decided to wait until Mr. Morganthal left; then I'd walk upstairs to ask Ned. I put my uniform on and showed the other ushers where to stand.

The girls arrived to work behind the candy counter, and the big arc light was flicked on, although it was not yet dark enough to really see it in the sky. Since the principal of our high school had also received an invitation to the premiere, Mr. Morganthal arranged for the Gaffney High School Band to stand outside the theater and play its repertoire of famous marches.

About eight o'clock, right after the band had finished playing "Onward Christian Soldiers" for the third straight time, the buses drove from the Veranda to the Palace, and the passengers entered the theater in high style. The men were dressed in tuxedos and black ties, and the women wore formal dresses and furs. Our town had never seen anything like it before, and the farmers, who had gathered all along Main Street with their wives and children, whistled and applauded as the audience entered. I was kept so busy ushering couples to their seats and making sure that the champagne was being served that I nearly forgot about Ned in the projection booth. My parents had arrived early and had taken two seats in the back row. My father kept asking, "What in the hell are we going to see, Edward?"

I went upstairs to ask Ned. "Hey, Ned, what's the film you got set up on the projector?"

"I'm not supposed to tell."

"Look, Ned, you can tell me. I'm the head usher."

"Mistah Morganthal say I ain't suppose to tell nobody." Ned just sat down on a three-legged stool and fanned himself with the *Gaffney Bulletin*. I looked around the booth, and Ned had a cot for himself set up in the corner. In a box by the projectors, the large metal containers that protected the films were opened. The label on one of them said *The Silence*.

"I promise I won't tell anyone, Ned."

"Will you bring me some champagne?"

"Yeah, Ned. What is it?"

"Some movie called *The Silence*. Swedish."

"What's it about?"

Ned just shrugged his shoulders and continued fanning himself. "Now you bring me up some champagne?"

"Yeah, I'll send somebody up with some."

"You ain't going to tell Mistuh Morganthal I told you?" Ned asked.

"No, I promise."

All the way back downstairs I was whistling to myself because Mr. Morganthal had brought a spy film. At least that's what I figured it out to be. *The Silence* didn't sound like a Western.

Along about eight-thirty, the mayor and his wife arrived, and Mr. Farley was beaming, showing off his teeth as if he had just bought them. He stopped in the lobby to say a few words to Mr. Morganthal about how glad he was to be invited and how good it was for Gaffney to have a movie theater once again. The mayor was confident that the Palace would draw much more business to the community. By then the Reverend Sayer and his wife came up, and all of them talked about how happy they were the Sunday mess had been straightened out.

The movie was scheduled to go on about eight forty-five, and so most of the people were settled when a last busload of people drove down Main Street and stopped outside the theater. On the bus must have been eight or so black people, all dressed to the hilt, in ties and top hats, carrying cigarette holders, and the women in formals and furs. When the citizens of Gaffney saw that, some of them nearly had a heart attack. One of the guys from the pool hall called out, "Hey, how come I'm not invited, but these niggers are?" The police hustled him away before any major disturbance broke out. When my friends and I started ushering the guests into the theater, the mayor nearly swallowed his cigar, but he didn't say anything. I knew he was fuming, though.

Mr. Morganthal, who was easily the best-dressed person there, with a well-fitted tuxedo, his short beard waxed and pointed, and a gold watch chain across his vest, told me to tell Ned to start the projector. He handed me a silver dollar. "For luck," he said. Ned was slightly drunk on the champagne, but not drunk enough to prevent him from working. He was lying on a cot when I opened the door to the projection booth.

"Mr. Morganthal says it's okay for you to start the projector."

"He want the cartoons or not?"

"He didn't tell me nothing, so I guess it's okay."

Up came the Donald Duck, and the house giggled and laughed with delight. I checked with my other ushers to see if everyone was properly seated, and then I took my station next to the rear door. I looked for my parents, but my eyes weren't used to the dark yet.

After the cartoon, the audience settled back in anticipation, and up came the main feature. It was in black and white, so a few members of the audience groaned. I could imagine my father telling my mother he wished it were in Technicolor. He could see black and white at home.

The title, *The Silence*, flashed across the screen, and then a bunch of Swedish names. Many of the words, such as producer, director, and actor were written in Swedish, and there were subtitles written underneath.

"Is this a foreign film?" the mayor whispered to his wife.

"I don't know. I ain't heard of none of those people before," she whispered. "Mrs. Robinson said it was going to be an Elizabeth Taylor film."

Mrs. Hendrix, the librarian, who was sitting next to my mother, whispered, "I didn't know I was going to have to read the movie." My mother giggled and placed her hand to her lips. The mayor, my parents, and their friends were all sitting in the last two rows, right by where I was standing. In fact, my father was at my elbow.

When the first scene came on, with a train load of tanks and a little boy traveling by train with two women, the audience became respectfully quiet. I went out in the lobby, where Mr. Morganthal was supervising the packing up of the champagne.

"Mr. Morganthal," I said.

"Yes Edward, what is it?"

"Is that a foreign film we're showing?"

"Look, be careful with those bottles, I don't want them broken," he told my friend Harvey Slater. "Yes, it's by Ingmar Bergman. You ought to stay in there and watch it. He's a great director. You can learn a lot about filmmaking from him."

"I've never seen a foreign film before."

"Phew!" Mr. Morganthal moved a case of champagne behind the counter and wiped his face with his silk handkerchief.

"I'm not so sure the people of Gaffney are going to like it," I said.

"They'll like it. It's a good film. Here, brush the dust off your uniform and go back in there in case you're needed. You can never tell when you'll be needed."

I went back inside and leaned against the door. On the screen, two women and a little boy were entering a hotel of some city, and the man in charge of the hotel spoke a language which nobody understood, most especially Mrs. Hendrix, who kept whispering to my mother, "What did he say? What did he say?" My father had already fallen asleep, leaning his head on his right hand. When he began to snore, someone in the row in front of him turned around and went "Shh! Shush." I nudged my father gently with my flashlight. "Uhh, uhh," he said.

"You're snoring," I whispered. I was glad that I had seated him next to the aisle.

He braced himself just in time to see one of the women on the screen beginning to undress. I could see that he was interested, but that he didn't want my mother to know. He shifted his weight uneasily in the chair, and uncrossed his legs.

"Stop fidgeting, and sit still," my mother whispered.

By now the woman on the screen was leaning over a sink, and there she was, washing her breasts in front of everyone. I leaned against the door and closed my eyes. I just knew what was going through my mother's mind.

"Do you want to go?" my father volunteered.

"Hush. Let's just see what kind of smut this Mr. Morganthal is peddling."

"This is what they call art nowadays," added Mrs. Hendrix.

"Oh my god!" It was the mayor, and he said it so loudly that everybody in the theater heard him. Alfred Branswik of the City Council, and a bachelor, placed his fingers in his mouth and whistled.

"Look, if you can't appreciate a good movie, why don't you leave?" someone responded. I fidgeted nervously and looked around for the other ushers. Here it was, our first day on the job, and now we were having a near riot on our hands.

"We are leaving. We're doing just that." Mrs. Sayer stood up and brandished her gloved fist toward the screen. "Those Swedes just don't have any pride at all. No sense of decency." The Reverend gravely stood up and silently followed his wife, although I noticed he kept looking back to see what was happening on the screen.

Alfred Branswik whistled again. "Hot dang, I didn't know this was going to be no stag film." I thought about telling him that I would have him thrown out if he continued to carry on, but since he was a member of the City Council I decided against it.

"I don't know what this world is coming to," Mrs. Hendrix told my mother. "Why I had a girl come in the other day and ask for a copy of *Peyton Place*. I told her we don't keep that trash on the shelf, and would she mind removing herself from the premises of the library."

"Shhh!" somebody said.

I was watching the Reverend and his wife, and, on their way to the aisle, Mrs. Sayer tripped over somebody's feet.

"Down in front!" Mr. Branswik hollered.

"She is down in front." That remark caused a great deal of laughter among the back rows. It was getting to be quite difficult to concentrate upon what was happening on the screen.

Now one of the women in the film was walking around with nothing on but her underpants. I looked to where my parents were sitting, and I was so embarrassed that I wanted the floor to open up and swallow me. The Reverend helped his wife up, and they barged past me, hardly giving me a chance to open the doors for them.

"'Night, Reverend," I said.

"Don't you goodnight us," Mrs. Sayer answered. I never seen her so mad before. Still I kept my eyes on the screen because I never saw nothing like it before, neither.

I thought my parents would follow the Reverend, but they didn't. My father was trying to convince my mother and Mrs. Hendrix that they should leave, but Mother insisted that they should see more, just to give the movie a chance. After all, it couldn't get any worse, she insisted. My father replied that he was getting a headache just trying to keep up with all the reading.

The friends of Mr. Morganthal's were pretty much taking it all in stride. Maybe because they were black, they were afraid to say something, or maybe because a lot were from Atlanta and had seen such things before.

From the lobby, I could overhear the Reverend and Mr. Morganthal discussing the film, so I went out there to see what was going on. "You really should give the movie more of a chance, Reverend."

"If I gave it any more of a chance, I wouldn't be able to stand before my congregation without blushing."

"Bergman is one of the finest directors in all of Europe."

"Smut peddler," said Mrs. Sayer, quite loudly. "That's what you mean."

"Well, Agnes," the Reverend added, attempting to calm his wife, "that might not be fair, since they do things differently in Sweden than they do in the United States."

"But do they have to do it right in front of us?"

"It's just not necessary to show such movies in our community. I'm sure there are far better films to be shown, Mr. Morganthal."

Mrs. Sayer tugged at her husband's elbow. "We hope all your films aren't going to be…going to be as…as…well like the one you have in there."

"I'm sorry you don't like the film," said Mr. Morganthal, stroking his beard. "I was hoping you would sit through the whole thing before judging it."

"I don't think that's at all necessary," answered Mrs. Sayers. "And I can't understand it. Your sister was such a proper lady."

"Yes. Well, it was a shame you and the Reverend never had time to visit her."

The Reverend put on his hat. "I'm afraid we must be going, Mr. Morganthal." The Reverend took his wife's arm, and together they walked quickly out onto the street. I glanced at Elizabeth, but we didn't say anything. I guess I was embarrassed for her too.

Mr. Morganthal shrugged his shoulders and smiled. I turned and slipped back inside the darkness before he saw me. My father had started to smoke a cigar, so I told him to put it out. It was a city ordinance.

"What about showing this?" he asked.

"What's happening?" somebody nearby asked.

"Do you understand there is a lot of symbolism in this picture," Mrs. Hendrix volunteered.

"Shhh!"

"Shhh!"

I silently prayed that the women on the screen would remain dressed for a while.

I don't know whether you've ever seen *The Silence* or not, but Ned Davis is of the opinion that it is about two spies trying to get information about a shipload of tanks. He may be right. Leastways I don't know, because I've only seen half of it, and probably not even the best half. But somewhere in that film is a scene where one of the women is alone with herself in bed, and she begins, well I heard someone using the phrase "touching herself," if you get what I mean, and that's where the roof fell in. The scene had barely gotten underway, when Mr. Bransik began whistling his head off, and two or three of the women stood up and angrily put on their things.

"Well I never!"

"How can decent people stand for this?"

Three or four champagne glasses shattered against the base of the stage, and Mr. Branswik whistled through his teeth. I wanted to rush down the aisle and restore order, but a hand grabbed the cap off my head and pushed me through the door. My mother had stiff-armed me, almost like a football player, and with her other arm, she pulled my half-awake father. I couldn't see Mrs. Hendrix, but I heard her murmuring. "Well I never saw such a thing in my life!"

"Let's get out of here, Maude."

"I want that man's license revoked," the mayor's wife said. In other aisles, about fifty or sixty of the most prominent citizens of Gaffney were making their exits.

"No daughter of mine is going to see a picture like that."

Mr. Morganthal came rushing to my aid, but it was too late. "Where are you going with my head usher?" he asked. He was mopping the sweat from his brow, but he still seemed calm, almost taking pleasure in the confusion.

"He may be or he *used to be* your head usher," my mother said, "but he's my son, and I won't have him work in a burlesque house."

"This is a movie theater, Mrs. Fields."

"Then why don't you show some decent movies?"

A crowd of citizens pushed past Mr. Morganthal, and a few of my friends had already been forced to leave.

"But I do have a decent movie up there," replied Mr. Morganthal softly.

My mother handed my usher's cap to Mr. Morganthal and told me to come along. "Come along, Edward," she said. "I'm not going to have any son of mine working here."

"Isn't your son old enough to decide that for himself, Mrs. Fields?"

"Not as long as he's living in my house and eating my cooking. If he wants to have a roof over his head tonight, he's coming with us."

"Mr. Morganthal… ," I started.

"Go along home, Edward. I'll send you your check." Mr. Morganthal walked over to the refreshment counter and placed my cap on top of the popcorn machine. I saw Elizabeth staring at me, so I turned away and ran out of the theater. I ran all the way home and locked myself in my room. I planned to join the army as quick as I could.

On Sunday it wasn't hard to guess what everybody was talking about, and my mother couldn't wait to tell her side of the story. The general consensus was that Mr. Morganthal would have to change his ways, or he would find himself in the bowels of hell.

That afternoon I heard that the Palace was packed with farm boys and with the regulars of the local pool hall, but that when they came out, they were angry about paying so much to see so little, though most of them sat through it to see the parts they wanted to see. I walked by the theater a couple of times, but I decided not to go in. I merely left my uniform with the Sunday ticket taker, and went home.

I haven't gone into the army yet, so mostly I'm working in the furniture factory for a buck-fifteen an hour, and keeping my eye on the latest developments at the Palace. After the grand opening, the Palace showed *Last Year at Marienbad* for about a week, then *La Dolce Vita* and *8 1/2*, and then a two-week festival of what Mr. Morganthal called underground films. I haven't gone to any of them, and I guess not too many people in Gaffney have, except maybe a few. What some people say is that if you want to go to meditate, you go to the Palace because it's quiet, and if you want entertainment, you go to church. On weekends, the farmers come in as usual and hang around the pool halls or the barbershop, and they just shake their heads at the whole thing. Sometimes the children ask to be taken to a movie, and so their parents still drive out to Star-Lite or they say, "We'll go next week when something good is playing," but next week comes, and nobody really goes. The theater still opens every day, though, and it has a three-dollar admission price.

I keep wanting to tell Mr. Morganthal that that ain't no way to run a theater, but I guess he really don't care. When he sent me my check for my day's work, he also sent me a lifetime free pass. I keep it in my wallet, and every once in a while, I'll look at it, but I don't care to go none. Maybe things will change when I go into the army. I hope so. I hope I get stationed somewhere near New York, because I know there are a lot of movie places there, but I guess nowhere is there a theater like the Palace. I bet there's no theater like it in the whole world. And I've got a lifetime pass to it. A lifetime pass to the Palace. And I don't even want to go.

*158*   **MUST I WEEP FOR THE DANCING BEAR**

# THE MAN WHO WAS STRUCK BY LIGHTNING

Every person of my generation remembers where he or she was and what he or she was doing when news about the assassination of President Kennedy reached them. Just as my parents remember the news surrounding the attack upon Pearl Harbor, my generation remembers the Zapruder film. We remember because there are not many moments when one's life blends so effortlessly and without seams into the larger life of our nation. For a brief period, we were part of a grand community of grief and were less alone. Our tears melded into the river called History. Surely, we thought a Revelation was at hand:

> *And the fourth angel sounded, and the third part of the sun was smitten, and the third part of the moon, and the third part of the stars: that the third part of them should be darkened, and the day should not shine for the third part of it, and the night in like manner.*

> *And I saw and I heard an eagle flying in mid-heaven, saying with a great voice, Woe, woe, woe for them that dwell on the earth....*

With woe, we passed from Camelot to the Great Society, carrying with us the knowledge that under the American Dream there was more violence than we realized to be reckoned with. At the time, of course, we could not know that the shots fired by Lee Harvey Oswald from the sixth floor of the Texas School Book Depository (think of the history books; think of all the knowledge in the world that might have been stored there) were signaling more assassinations to come, that the bullets ended nothing but a life, but a life that would resonate, its reputation built upon unfinished business, unfulfilled dreams, that the assassination was merely and profoundly a 6.5 mail-order Italian-carbine preamble to other deaths and more unfinished business. How unfair, we thought. How unjust that History gives equal weight to good and to evil. Someone from nowhere, a fully accredited three-named summa-cum-laude loser could shove open the door of our collective memories by pointing a gun out of a high window and shattering a life.

Bang. Bang. Bang. John B. Connally took the second bullet, but in the history of the world, the wounded don't count. I am wounded, and you are wounded. But how much do we count? We don't count. We live and we remember. We remember that fateful day in much the same way we cherish the day or night in which we offered up, as in a sacrifice, our frail and only virginity. Indeed we remember, remember with regret and hope, the loss of innocence. Bang. Bang. Bang.

• • • •

I am thinking all this because I am sitting in an art gallery watching a professor of philosophy from Miami-Dade Junior College show his slides: black-and-white photographs of poor people, the down-and-out of Manhattan, the flophouse award winners, Haitian refugees, wino express-card holders, bag ladies, Academy Award winners for best supporting roles in the motion picture *Drunk*. When I first knew him, the philosopher/photographer, he was neither a philosopher nor a photographer. He was a graduate student in art history at the same Baptist college in the South I had been attending. I wasn't a Baptist. My parents had no money, and so I went to the first college that offered me a scholarship. My girlfriend, who later became my wife, or at least my first wife in this world of woe and serial polygamy, was studying flute at the aforesaid self-same college. She and I had been visiting the philosopher-to-be in his apartment when the radio announced that President Kennedy had been wounded in Dallas and had been rushed to the hospital. (Did thinking about the assassination drive him into philosophy?) Mattie started to cry. I felt a terrible chill. To be certain that we had heard the news correctly, we walked across the campus in search of friends. Her eyes were swollen from all her crying. Years later she would cry that much again.

One by one, slides vanished from the screen. The photographer and I had been invited back to our alma mater for Homecoming. There was light falling through the window. In the art gallery, there were only a few of us in the audience. One woman was a former teacher of mine; she had brought her sister. My former teacher, who was now nearing seventy years of age, reminded me how I left a term paper inside her refrigerator. I had written a paper for her course in linguistics. When I went to her house to deliver it, she and her husband were absent. Although there was no one at home, the house was unlocked. They were trusting people. I walked in, opened the refrigerator door, and propped the paper up between two quart cartons of milk. She got a big laugh out of that. So did I. Twenty years later, and there we were talking about it; and twenty years later I was watching the photographs of a man whom Mattie and I had been visiting the day Kennedy was shot. Had that been the last time I had seen the philosopher/photographer in two decades?

There was a lady huddled against the white tiles of a stucco building in Miami. She was a black lady with skin like leather. Her arms were folded across her chest. She was in pain. There was pain everywhere. In the terminology of the art world, there is the word *grisaille.* It is a style of painting that uses only gray tints and gives the effect of sculpture in relief. Perhaps the term was not appropriate to photography, but it came to mind as I looked at the slides. His photographs showed the parts of things in black and white. I thought that my life consisted of several parts. Memory was just one of those parts. Do we remember our lives in color or in black and white? Grisaille.

At the Student Union Building, my American Studies professor was standing by the switchboard. He was waiting for news. His face was streaked with tears. Everybody was crying. Well, not everybody. My ex-roommate from my freshman year, a fat boy from Jacksonville, wasn't upset in the least. He was gleeful. Later that night, when the death of Kennedy was a certainty, there were stories of parties being thrown, parties in the dorms, parties celebrating the death of Kennedy. Nobody loves everybody all the time.

Chirico. The painter born in Greece. Giorgio de Chirico. It wasn't fair, but the photographs in stark black and white reminded me of Chirico.

Classes were cancelled. My religion professor mentioned the Apocalypse. Bergman's *The Seventh Seal* had been shown on campus the week before:

> *And when he opened the seventh seal,*
> *there followed a silence in heaven about*
> *the space of half an hour.*

During the next few days, we watched the funeral on television. Behind the coffin of the President trotted a horse that had no rider. The riderless horse haunted my dreams for several weeks:

> *And I saw the heaven opened; and*
> *behold a white horse, and he that sat*
> *thereon called Faithful and True; and in*

*righteousness he doth judge and make*
*war. And his eyes are a flame of fire.*

Once you've been to a Baptist college, there are some things you never get out of your blood. The Book of Revelation is one. War on earth. War in heaven. Rumors were endless. If the Russians had killed John Kennedy, we would have had to go to war. There would be no choice.

In life, we had stuck by Kennedy during the Cuban Missile Crisis. We had sat glued to the television set and thought that at any moment World War III would erupt. Parents had called their daughters and sons home. After all, we were in Florida and not far away from the main stage of impending disaster. My theater teacher used to drive his family to Texas so that his children could stay with their grandparents. That didn't seem logical to me, but when are our lives ruled by logic?

If we could stick with Kennedy to the brink of war during his lifetime, we could march into Moscow after his death. Millions more would be killed. We would pry open the oyster of a single death and bring forth the pearl of atomic destruction. Don't think it wasn't on our minds. We were frightened. Every last one of us. Overnight, we had become political scientists. The FBI and the CIA could have recruited any of us. All of us were around-the-clock detectives. We had our theories and our sources. Years later the bookstores would be flooded with conspiracy theories. We had seen Jack Ruby kill Lee Harvey Oswald. What did that mean? What did it all mean? We were walking around in a nightmare. Hour by hour, television held out an electronic tit to our hungry mouths. The breasts of NBC, ABC, and CBS were far-reaching. Never had so many victims and victimizers become so famous so fast. And more than once we were reminded how quickly we were being fed. When Abraham Lincoln was assassinated by John Wilkes Booth, some persons living in the mountains of the Far West did not receive the news until nearly a year later. To allow citizens to partake in the community of grief, Lincoln's funeral train paused at numerous small towns, where citizens wept, sang, and marched.

We did not sing. We did not march. We stayed home and watched the parade of events on television.

The image of the riderless horse did not leave me, but it was not all that I dreamt. I approached a green house. It was, in effect a private club. Perhaps I was being invited to become a member. A famous writer greeted me at the door. He was famous, but I did not know who he was, nor had I read any of his books. So much for fame. Instead of exploring the private griefs of the human heart, he would have been better off if he had gone out and shot someone. He could then sell his life story to the movies. Perhaps he had something like that in mind, because he exhibited two miniature alligators. The author smeared me with blood. He rubbed blood on my face, blood on my bare arms. The miniature alligators came alive at the smell of blood. The object was this: I was to hide somewhere, and the alligators would seek me out. My wife-to-be was there. She was shocked at the author's behavior, but was powerless to stop it. I remembered where the bathroom was. I ran there to wash the blood off, but the blood would not rub off. Later, my American Studies professor sought me out. He had abandoned his post at the switchboard. He was very kind to me. He kept asking me did I have enough money? Was I all right? My answer in both cases was No.

The photographer said you don't need any big philosophy to take pictures. Just take pictures of things that interest you. Unfortunately, it takes an entire lifetime to find out what interests you. Who can ever forget the photo of Lee Harvey Oswald taking the bullet from Jack Ruby? Up came a slide of the black man who had been struck by lightning. And then it all came back to me.

At 1:00 p.m. the doctors at Parkland Memorial Hospital pronounced the President dead. When the New York Stock Exchange closed down trading at eighteen minutes to two, it had absorbed a loss of fifteen billion dollars. The loss that the rest of us absorbed was not so easily measurable.

My wife-to-be and I abandoned the Student Union Building

and its weeping hordes. We drifted into town. In a shanty near the Greyhound Bus Station lived a black man who worked as a janitor in our dorms. His claim to fame was that he had been struck by lightning three times and had lived to tell about it. The first time he was standing out in the yard by his house. He was only eleven years old. The bolt of lightning broke out all the windows in his house and knocked him flat to the earth. The second time he had been fishing on the St. John's River, and the lightning crackled up and down the zippers of his raincoat. The third time he was caddying on the local golf course. The overdose of electricity burnt his eyebrows off and did terrible things to his brain. He had a difficult time remembering. Sometimes he would speak and no words came out.

We found Simon sitting on his porch. He hated mankind with a vengeance, but he didn't mind me. I had been trying to teach him to read and write. It was my small blow against the injustices of society, my contribution to creating a great society. The Peace Corps at home. I had been wasting my time. Simon would never learn to read and write. However, he appreciated my interest. He tolerated my wife-to-be because she was a musician. Simon played the guitar and harmonica, and sometimes Mattie and he would play duets. He was sitting on the porch, all 200 pounds of him. He was wearing khaki pants and a white undershirt.

"Did you hear the news?" I asked him. I stood on the street and didn't cross into his yard without an invitation. Black and white didn't mix too well at our school. He was the only black man even near the college.

"What news?" He placed a hand behind his right ear. With his left hand, he waved us toward the porch. Two chickens and a rooster pecked in a yard littered with tires and broken glass.

"President Kennedy has been shot," I said.

"He's dead," Mattie added.

Simon brought out a pitcher of lemonade. "Who was it that you said died?" he asked.

"President Kennedy," Mattie told him.

"Oh yeah. I'd better write that down so I don't forget it."

But he couldn't write it down, so I wrote it down for him. Printed it, actually. In block letters on a tiny piece of white paper. A cash register receipt from Woolworth's.

"I knew lots of mens who killed mens, but I never knew noone to kill the President." Simon poured out the lemonade. The Greyhound buses were going down the street, going somewhere. But no bus was going so far away that it was beyond killing and poverty. "I was struck by lightning three times," he announced proudly. "They should make me President because I was struck by lightning three times. God picked me out for some special purpose. He could have had me killed any one of those times. The President is struck by a bullet and he dead. I am hit by lightning and I alive. That make sense to you?"

"It doesn't make sense to me," I told him.

We drank the lemonade, and Mattie put the glasses in the kitchen. When we left, Simon stood up and waved his flyswatter. "Now what was it you come to tell me?" he asked. "Something about somebody being dead."

"I just wanted you to know about the radio," I told him.

"Mine's busted," he said.

"I know."

"It wasn't a black man what did it?" he asked. He put his hand behind his right ear.

"No," I said. "It wasn't a black man."

He nodded and sat back down, pushing his harmonica back and forth across the table. "That's good. If it'd been a black man, that would be a trouble. A lot of trouble." He thought about what he said and rubbed his eyes. "More trouble than anyone of us know how to handle." He picked up his harmonica and held it tightly like the treasure it was. "You wrote his name down for me, didn't you?"

I told him I had, but he couldn't read the printing anyway.

Simon didn't respond. He motioned us to sit down. His front porch had five green chairs on it, five iron chairs. When you placed your arms down on the arm rests, you came away with flecks of rust.

"Radio's busted," Simon said.

"A man took a rifle and shot the President," I told him.

"In Dallas," Mattie added.

"I don't have no radio," Simon said, nodding his head up and down.

"You can come over to the dorm," I told him. The three of us sat on the front porch looking out at the street of sunlight. The chickens and the rooster never stopped their pecking. The sunlight glittered off the broken glass. The thing to do was to buy a bottle of Coke at the Greyhound Station, and toss the empty into Simon's yard. It didn't matter to him, and he collected the deposit.

"You can come over to the dorm and watch it on the television set."

"Don't want to watch it," Simon said. "Don't want to hear about it." He kept his false teeth in the house. They bothered him something awful, he said. That's why he took them out the moment he got home. When he spoke without his teeth, it was hard to understand him. He mumbled. He mumbled and he told a lot of lies. Lies made his life more interesting, I figured. Lies made his life more intelligible. He was fifty years old and he spent his whole life near the Greyhound station. He watched the buses roll in and the buses roll out, but he never went anywhere himself. His wife was dead. His children had moved away. His hands were huge and calloused.

"Did a black man do it?"

"A white man," I told him again. "Lee Harvey Oswald."

He looked at Mattie. She was wearing sunglasses, not because of the bright sunlight, but because of her swollen eyes. "People are always killing somebody," he said.

"Yeah," I agreed. "But not the President. Not the President of the United States. Not in 1963. This is not the Stone Age."

"Ain't my President," he said. "Ain't my President. White folks' President. White folks nominate the President. White folks elect the President. White folks shoot the President." He picked up a flyswatter and made a half-hearted attempt to kill a worrisome fly.

"He was doing his best," Mattie said.

"I do my best, too." Simon said, not looking at us, just watching the chickens. "I do my best, but I don't have a radio that works."

"Want my radio?" I asked.

He shook his head. "I don't want nothing that not mine."

"It could be yours."

"I don't want nothing that not mine."

He went in the house and brought out his harmonica and his guitar. Mattie took the guitar. They played some spirituals. I listened and watched the chickens, and counted the Coke bottles in the yard. We had a game we played with Coke bottles. When we bought bottles from a machine, we would look on the bottoms of the bottles to see where the bottles came from. The person who held the bottle from the farthest away place won the game. I never held a Coke bottle from Dallas.

# About The Author

Louis Phillips is a widely published poet, playwright, and short story writer. He has written some 45 books for children and adults. His sequence of poems *—The Time, The Hour, The Solitariness of the Place* —was the co-winner in the Swallow's Tale Press competition (1984). Among his published books of poems are: *The Krazy Kat Rag* (Light Reprint Press), *Bulkington* (Hollow Spring Press), *The Time, The Hour, The Solitariness of the Place* (Swallow's Tale Press ). Among his works are: four collections of short stories—*A Dream of Countries Where No One Dare Live* (SMU Press), *The Bus to the Moon* (Fort Schuyler Press), and *The Woman Who Wrote 'King Lear,' and Other Stories* (Pleasure Boat Studio), and, most recently, *Fireworks in Some Particulars* (Fort Schuyler Press). He teaches at the School of Visual Arts in NYC.

"Versatility is not Phillips' sole virtue as a writer. Varied as his characters are, he can sketch a protagonist with a few deft lines. defining him so clearly that whatever happens next, no matter how odd, seems right." – Amanda Heller, in *The Boston Globe*

"If you can imagine the world which might have resulted had Bernard Malamud and Flannery O'Connor collaborated, then you can understand the country that Louis Phillips runs through." - Laura Kennelly, *Grasslands Review*

# How We Got Our Name

…from *Pleasure Boat Studio,* an essay written by Ouyang Xiu, Song Dynasty poet, essayist, and scholar, on the twelfth day of the twelfth month in the renwu year (January 25, 1043):

"I have heard of men of antiquity who fled from the world to distant rivers and lakes and refused to their dying day to return. They must have found some source of pleasure there. If one is not anxious for profit, even at the risk of danger, or is not convicted of a crime and forced to embark; rather, if one has a favorable breeze and gentle seas and is able to rest comfortably on a pillow and mat, sailing several hundred miles in a single day, then is boat travel not enjoyable? Of course, I have no time for such diversions. But since 'pleasure boat' is the designation of boats used for such pastimes, I have now adopted it as the name of my studio. Is there anything wrong with that?"

Translated by Ronald Egan

# Books from Pleasure Boat Studio: A Literary Press

*Note: Other PBS imprints - Caravel, Aequitas, and Empty Bowl - are not included in this list*

*Must I Weep for the Dancing Bear, And Other Stories* • *Louis Phillips* • $16

*Taos Mountain* • Robert Sund • poetry and paintings • casebound • $45

*Notes from Disappearing Lake* • Robert Sund • poetry • $15

*Path to the Sea* • Liliana Ursu, trans. from Romanian by Tess Gallagher and Adam Sorkin • poems •     $15.95

*Songs from a Yahi Bow: A Series of Poems about Ishi* • poems by Mike O'Connor, Scott Ezell, and Yusef Komunyakaa, with an essay by Thomas Merton and paintings by Jeff Hengst • $15

*Goodbye, Philip Roth* • Martin Smith • fiction • $14.95

*Toys in My Attic* • Russell Connor • humor • $13.95

*Beautiful Passing Lives* • Ed Harkness • poems • $15

*Immortality* • Mike O'Connor • poems • $16

*Painting Brooklyn Stories* • Paintings by Nina Talbot, Poetry by Esther Cohen • $20

*Ghost Farm* • Pamela Stewart • poems • $13

*Unknown Places* • Peter Kantor, trans. from Hungarian by Michael Blumenthal • poems • $14

*Leaving Yesler* • Peter Bacho • fiction • $16

*Moonlight in the Redemptive Forest* • Michael Daley • poems (includes a CD) • $16

*Jew's Harp* • Walter Hess • poems • $14

*God Is a Tree, and Other Middle-Age Prayers* • Esther Cohen • poems • $10

*The Light on Our Faces* • Lee Whitman-Raymond • poems • $13

*Crossing the Water: The Hawaii-Alaska Trilogies* • Irving Warner • fiction • $16

*Unnecessary Talking: The Montesano Stories* • Mike O'Connor • fiction • $16

*Home & Away: The Old Town Poems* • Kevin Miller • $15

*Craving Water* • Mary Lou Sanelli • poems • $15

*Weinstock Among the Dying* • Michael Blumenthal • fiction • $18

*The War Journal of Lila Ann Smith* • Irving Warner • historical fiction • $18

*Dream of the Dragon Pool: A Daoist Quest* • Albert A. Dalia • fantasy • $18

*Monique* • Luisa Coehlo, trans. fm Portuguese by Maria do Carmo de Vasconcelos and Dolores DeLuise • fiction • $14

*Against Romance* • Michael Blumenthal • poetry • $14

*Artrage* • Everett Aison • fiction • $15

*Days We Would Rather Know* • Michael Blumenthal • poems • $14

*Wagner, Descending: The Wrath of the Salmon Queen* • Irving Warner • fiction • $16

*Schilling, from a study in lost time* • Terrell Guillory • fiction • $17

*The Enduring Vision of Norman Mailer* • Dr. Barry H. Leeds • criticism • $18

*The Immigrant's Table* • Mary Lou Sanelli • poems and recipes • $14

*When the Tiger Weeps* • Mike O'Connor • poetry and prose • $15

*Nature Lovers* • Charles Potts • poems • $10

*Puget Sound: 15 Stories* • C. C. Long • stories • $14

*Concentricity* • Sheila E. Murphy • poems • $13.95

*Rumours: A Memoir of a British POW in WWII* • Chas Mayhead • nonfiction • $16

*Another Life, and Other Stories* • Edwin Weihe • stories • $16

*Women in the Garden* • Mary Lou Sanelli • poems • $14

*The Eighth Day of the Week* • Alfred Kessler • fiction • $16

*If You Were With Me Everything Would Be All Right* • Ken Harvey • stories • $16

*Pronoun Music* • Richard Cohen • stories • $16

*Saying the Necessary* • Edward Harkness • poems • $14

*Setting Out: The Education of Li-li* • Tung Nien • Translated from Chinese by Mike O'Connor • $15

*In Memory of Hawks, & Other Stories from Alaska* • Irving Warner • stories • $15

*When History Enters the House: Essays from Central Europe* • Michael Blumenthal • $15

*The Politics of My Heart* • William Slaughter • poems • $13

*The Rape Poems* • Frances Driscoll • poems • $13

*Setting Out: The Education of Lili* • Tung Nien • trans. fm Chinese by Mike O'Connor • fiction • $15

Our Chapbook Series:

No. 1: *The Handful of Seeds: Three and a Half Essays* • Andrew Schelling • $7 • nonfiction

No. 2: *Original Sin* • Michael Daley • $8 • poetry

No. 3: *Too Small to Hold You* • Kate Reavey • $8 • poetry

No. 4: *The Light on Our Faces* – re-issued in non-chapbook (see above list)

No. 5: Eye • William Bridges • $8 • poetry

No. 6: *Selected* New Poems *of Rainer Maria Rilke* • trans. fm German by Alice Derry • $10 • poetry

No. 7: *Through High Still Air: A Season at Sourdough Mountain* • Tim McNulty • $9 • poetry, prose

No. 8: *Sight Progress* • Zhang Er, trans. fm Chinese by Rachel Levitsky • $9 • prosepoems

No. 9: *The Perfect Hour* • Blas Falconer • $9 • poetry

No. 10: *Fervor* • Zaedryn Meade • $10 • poetry

No. 11: *Some Ducks* • Tim McNulty • $10 • poetry

No. 12: *Late August* • Barbara Brackney • $10 • poetry

No. 13: *The Right to Live Poetically* • Emily Haines • $9 • poetry


*Orders*: Pleasure Boat Studio books are available by order from your bookstore, directly from our website, or through the following:

**SPD** (Small Press Distribution) Tel. 8008697553, Fax 5105240852

**Partners/West** Tel. 4252278486, Fax 4252042448

**Baker & Taylor** 8007751100, Fax 8007757480

**Ingram** Tel 6157935000, Fax 6152875429

**Amazon.com** or **Barnesandnoble.com**


Pleasure Boat Studio: A Literary Press

201 West 89th Street

New York, NY 10024

Tel / Fax: 8888105308

www.pleasureboatstudio.com / pleasboat@nyc.rr.com